THE SURVIVALIST

#22

BRUTAL CONQUEST

Books by Jerry Ahern

The Survivalist Series

#1: Total War
#2: The Nightmare Begins
#3: The Quest
#4: The Doomsayer
#5: The Web
#6: The Savage Horde
#7: The Prophet
#8: The End is Coming
#9: Earth Fire
#10: The Awakening
#11: The Reprisal
#12: The Rebellion
#13: Pursuit
#14: The Terror
#15: Overlord

Mid-Wake
#16: The Arsenal
#17: The Ordeal
#18: The Struggle
#19: Final Rain
#20: Firestorm
#21: To End All War
The Legend
#22: Brutal Conquest
#23: Call To Battle
#24: Blood Assassins
#25: War Mountain
#26: Countdown
#27: Death Watch

The Defender Series

#1: The Battle Begins
#2: The Killing Wedge
#3: Out of Control
#4: Decision Time
#5: Entrapment
#6: Escape

#7: Vengeance
#8: Justice Denied
#9: Deathgrip
#10: The Good Fight
#11: The Challenge
#12: No Survivors

They Call Me the Mercenary Series

#1: The Killer Genesis
#2: The Slaughter Run
#3: Fourth Reich Death Squad
#4: The Opium Hunter
#5: Canadian Killing Ground
#6: Vengeance Army
#7: Slave of the Warmonger
#8: Assassin's Express
#9: The Terror Contract

#10: Bush Warfare
#11: Death Lust!
#12: Headshot!
#13: Naked Blade, Naked Gun
#14: The Siberian Alternative
#15: The Afghanistan Penetration
#16: China Bloodhunt
#17: Buckingham Blowout

THE SURVIVALIST

#22

BRUTAL CONQUEST

JERRY AHERN

SPEAKING VOLUMES, LLC
NAPLES, FLORIDA
2013

THE SURVIVALIST
#22 BRUTAL CONQUEST

ISBN 978-1-61232-281-0

*To the men and women of Operation Desert Shield,
allies against tyranny and greed in man's oldest quest, for
justice.*

Chapter One

A lightning bolt struck the engine of the helicopter's main rotor, and an alarm sounded instantly. Nearly as quickly, the wailing of the Klaxon was lost beneath the screams of the just-rescued women. More lightning bolts and raw plasma energy in the form of ball lightning surrounded them, the sky ripping open in a torrent of rain. The storm was upon them before there was time to think, time to react, or time to take any form of evasive action.

"We are going down!" Natalia screamed, barely audible over the shrieks of the freed captives of the Land Pirates.

John Rourke pushed to his feet, Michael a step ahead of him. Rourke shouted to Paul and Annie, "Try to keep these women calm so we can hear ourselves think. Get them into crash positions. Hurry!"

There was a droning sound, the rush of the slipstream along the fuselage. Then another lightning strike, one of the overhead electrical panels catching fire. Michael grabbed a bulkhead-mounted extinguisher, shouting to the freed captives, "Get back! I've gotta put the fire out! Get back!"

John Rourke pushed past his son, into the Eden gunship's cockpit.

All around them there was green-tinged blackness. "It was just here, John! A moment ago, it was clear all around us. Then we were into the storm. We still have tail rotor control, but I don't know how much longer! We're going to crash."

John Rourke reached around her, grabbing for the joystick. It moved too easily. "Damnit." Freezing rain and hail enveloped them, one of the overhead cockpit bubble panels cracking, spider-webbing under the repeated impact from balls of ice that were nearly the size of baseballs.

Rourke lurched into the copilot's seat beside her, buckling in as he started hitting switches on the auxiliary control panel. His hand closed over hers on the joystick, feeling for a response from the controls. There was none.

"I was terrain following to avoid a lightning strike, but it did not—"

Rourke interrupted her. The snow-and ice-splotched floor of the rift valley, jagged upthrusting slabs of rock and mounds of rilled dirt everywhere, was coming up fast. "Can you still control the tail at all, Natalia?"

"Not enough. Hold on."

John Rourke's mind raced, searching for a solution, but there was none. He braced as he shouted aft, "Impact's coming up! Brace yourselves!"

There was a moment when all motion seemed to stop, then everything around them shook and the helicopter was skidding along the ground, starting to turn over.

"All fuel supply systems are off," Natalia shouted.

Rourke braced his hands against the overhead as the helicopter flipped forward. There were screams.

The smell of synth-fuel.

The smell of insulation burning.

The helicopter turned onto its side, blades from the main rotor slicing past them along the ground, shattering the chin bubble.

There was a blur of motion, something long and black rocketing past them, a portion of the portside bulkhead peeling away, the tail rotor spinning along the ground, churning a furrow into the dirt and snow before it smashed against a rock and broke up.

Then all motion stopped.

John Rourke hung over the right side of the copilot's seat, a piece of one of the main rotor blades, twisted and gnarled, punched through the chin bubble inches from his left leg.

He looked up and to his left.

Natalia, unmoving, hung suspended from her seat restraint.

John Rourke reached for the quick release buckle of his harness but it was jammed. The smell of burning insulation was even stronger now. He shook his head to clear it.

"How is it back there?" Rourke called aft.

His daughter Annie's voice shouted back, "Some injuries. I don't think anyone's dead."

John Rourke had the little A.G. Russell Sting IA Black Chrome in his hand, and was using it to cut through the webbing of the seat restraint.

He was finished with the section that passed over his left shoulder, and was starting on the piece still secured around his waist. "Natalia? Answer me! Come on! Wake up, Natalia!"

She moved her head and shook it. "We are—"

"—alive. This thing's on fire and we've got to get out in order to stay alive. Think! Come on!"

She shook her head again. "I . . . uhh . . ."

Rourke had cut through the other section of seat restraint, putting his knife in his teeth as he twisted out of the seat and reached up toward Natalia. Her seat restraint release buckle worked, and as he activated it, she fell from the pilot's seat and into his arms.

Rourke held her for an instant. He loved her. He always would. But he loved his wife. Natalia was Michael's woman now. And although he would never stop loving her, he was happy for them . . . for both of them.

Natalia's eyelids fluttered as he set her down against the side of the copilot's seat. As he sheathed his little knife, he gazed at the incredible blueness of her eyes. "Can you walk?" Rourke asked.

"Yes. I—" She shook her head and closed her eyes. "I am all right. Help the others."

Rourke pulled her to her feet and she swayed against him, then he pushed her aft, ducking her head down for her as she turned sideways to get through.

7

There was smoke here, dense and acrid smelling. Michael, his head bleeding, was handing some of the injured women out of the main compartment and up to Paul and Annie, who hung down through where the portside fuselage door had been, now a jagged tear.

There was a hole in the overhead, now to Rourke's left because the craft was turned on its side, where the main rotor assembly had been sheared away.

Martin, the neo-Nazi leader of Eden, the son taken from John and Sarah in the instant of birth, pushed past one of the injured women and started to clamber up toward the opening where Paul and Annie were. John Rourke straight-armed Martin in the chest, spinning him around. "Help with these people. Now, damnit!"

"Let them all die! They will anyway."

John Rourke grabbed Martin by the front of his shirt. "Help them or you'll die." He pushed Martin away.

Martin reached down to one of the women. She visibly recoiled from him. But he grabbed her up, starting to hand her out to Paul and Annie.

Rourke's eyes scanned the cabin. Despite the smoke, the recurrent lightning flashes allowed him to see clearly enough. And red panic lights glowed from some of the bulkhead and overhead receptacles, others blown out or shattered.

There was a woman with a piece of shrapnel sticking through her left arm. Rourke pushed away debris, dropped to his knees, and quickly set to work. He had to free her arm from the shrapnel—a piece of the fuselage body twisted inward—before he could carry her out.

The smoke was getting thicker. As he braced his left knee against her left shoulder, then grasped her arm to raise it off the metal spike, he told her, "I'm a doctor. You'll be all right."

He only hoped he was right.

"Tell me your blood type, in case you pass out."

"I—"

"Blood type. Come on. O, AB, what?"

8

"O positive, I think."

"Good girl. Don't be afraid to scream. It'll help." He took a glove from his pocket and put it between her teeth. "Bite. Now!"

He pulled.

She screamed, but the scream died in her throat as the pain put her into unconsciousness. But he had her free. He reached to his snow smock, ripping away the left sleeve at the shoulder, then turning it inside out and twisting it, binding it above her wound as a tourniquet.

"I've got the medical kit they had in here. All our stuff's out," Michael was shouting.

"Get Martin out of here and tell Annie to keep an eye on him. If he runs, kneecap him."

"Right."

"Get Natalia out. Get her to sit down someplace. Might be concussion. What about the rest of the women?"

"All of them out. No dead."

"This one will need a transfusion. Find somebody with O positive and see if you can scrounge up some fuel line or something for the transfusion."

"Right."

"How's your head?" John Rourke had the woman bandaged and was staunching the flow of blood.

"Just a scratch, but it's bleeding a lot. I'm fine."

"Head wounds can be serious. I'll take a look in a minute." Rourke looked back over his shoulder. Martin was scrambling out, and Michael was helping Natalia into Paul's hands. He pulled her up and she was out.

Then Michael dropped to one knee beside John Rourke and the injured woman. "I'll give you a hand."

"All right. Take that side. Watch her arm." They lifted her between them, John Rourke shouting to Paul, "Give us a hand."

They pushed the woman up as Paul extended his hands, grabbing her left side, holding her as Michael eased himself up and out through the opening. John Rourke pushed upward on the woman's body, and Paul and Michael had her.

9

Rourke took a quick glance around the cabin.

"Michael! Paul!"

"Yeah?" It was Paul's voice.

"Sure you have everything?"

"Everything, Dad," Michael called down.

John Rourke nodded, coughing as he inhaled too deeply and swallowed too much smoke.

He reached up, grabbed a handhold, and started to wrestle himself clear, Michael's and Paul's hands on his shoulders and upper arms, pulling him up.

Rourke jumped down into the snow.

The rain still fell, icy sleet, hailstones pelting the ground, striking his face. He pulled up the hood of his parka.

The women, Martin Zimmer, Natalia, and Annie were already about thirty yards from the craft.

Michael and Paul jumped down, and together the three of them started away from the helicopter as quickly as they could. There was no telling if or when it would explode, and the fact that it hadn't as of yet was no guarantee it wouldn't in the next second.

"What'll we do now, John?" Paul shouted over the keening of the wind and the hammering of the rain.

"Remember the old joke? 'What you mean *we*, paleface?' Well, I don't know yet. We need shelter. Was there a survival kit—"

And then the roar started, John Rourke grabbing his son and his friend, pushing them down into the snow as he threw himself between them.

The helicopter.

The noise of the explosion was painfully loud. There was a rush of heat. Rourke covered his head and neck with his forearms, trying to shelter his bare hands. Debris rained down around them, some of it burning.

Michael's parka caught fire. John Rourke rolled his son over, shouting, "Your coat!" Michael smothered the fire and got to his knees.

John Rourke stood up, looking back.

All that remained of the gunship now was a skeleton. Its

missile pods were still in place, but the wiring was fused. Fortunately, none of the missiles detonated.

His ears still rang a little from the explosion as Paul, standing beside him, said, "In answer to your question, yes."

John Rourke looked at him.

"A survival kit. Probably has some sort of shelter in it, but can't be much."

The rain was starting to slacken, and overhead the electrical activity was subsiding, the sky lightening.

Michael stood at his father's side. "They're going to be coming, Dad."

John Rourke just nodded.

Mentally, he began making a list of what had to be done, in order of importance.

The woman with the blood loss from the wounded arm. And the other injured had to be tended to. The shelter, if there was one, could be erected to protect the more seriously injured. Meanwhile, there was the question of exposure.

"Shit," John Rourke almost whispered.

Paul Rubenstein clapped him on the shoulder, saying, "Took the word right off the tip of my tongue, John. What the hell are we going to do with these people? I mean, where do we take them?"

"Find a cave . . . something. No time to talk, gentlemen." John Rourke turned away from the wreckage and started jogging through the rocks and snow and slush.

Chapter Two

Paul had scavenged a fuel line, and after cleaning and disinfecting it, Rourke transfused little more than a pint of blood from three women among the group rescued from the stronghold of the Land Pirates, not wishing to weaken any of the donors seriously enough to affect survivability under the extreme conditions surrounding them.

As long as Martin Zimmer was a prisoner, there would not be an outright attack by the Land Pirates or the Eden armed forces, but it was inevitable that some of the massive mobile fortresses were coming through the rift valley even now, in pursuit. Their radar might have sufficient range to have detected the crash, which meant they would be coming all the faster.

Natalia had been airborne for roughly thirty minutes. Rourke calculated that they had covered perhaps fifty miles, maybe as many as sixty.

Maximum speed for the fortresses — multi-treaded massive armored vehicles with main decks Paul estimated to be nearly the size of a football field — could be no more than thirty miles per hour flat out over good terrain, unless Rourke seriously misjudged their capabilities. In the rift valley, half that speed for vehicles of that size would be hard to maintain. But at fifteen miles per hour, considering flight time and the time already spent tending the injured, the first of the fortresses would be coming into sight in two to three hours.

Without shelter, he'd start losing some of the women to exposure in half that time. The women, having been kidnapped by the Land Pirates from communities throughout the Wildlands, were already malnourished, and were dressed in little better than rags, ill suited for survival in the sub-freezing temperatures.

John Rourke's parka, along with those of the others, was already gone, as were the Eden uniform parts worn by Paul and Annie and Natalia. The snow pants were given over to be used as best they could for jackets.

The last of the serious wounds attended to, John Rourke stepped out of the four-man shelter and into the blast, only a heavy military-style sweater over his ordinary clothing.

It was late morning, the sky grey and threatening, but the storm that had almost literally shot them out of the sky was gone.

Rourke rubbed his hands over his upper arms for circulation.

Annie, back in her own clothes but minus her parka, stood shivering, holding a gun on Martin Zimmer.

Martin Zimmer. John Rourke took one of the thin, dark tobacco cigars from a pocket beneath his sweater, the end already cut off, then clamped it between his teeth. He walked toward Michael and Paul, who were sorting the gear from the aircraft into relatively equal loads. They even had the door gun and two boxes of link belt cartridges. He joined them, his son and his best friend. Martin Zimmer. It was clear now that Deitrich Zimmer, the brilliant micro-surgeon and geneticist, had planned very well, up to and including faking his own death as well as that of the newborn child he had kidnapped.

Zimmer had a brother Jurgen, a confirmed neo-Nazi like Deitrich himself, dedicated to establishing a new world order. However dedicated Jurgen Zimmer had been, though, John Rourke seriously doubted the man had volunteered himself as a corpse to substitute for Deitrich. But it had to have been Jurgen Zimmer's body that, along with a look-alike for Commander Dodd, had

13

been discovered in the wreckage of a helicopter crash.

Unlike Dodd, Commander of the Eden Project shuttle fleet, who was born in the Twentieth Century before the process really progressed out of the experimental stage, there was a genetic fingerprint of Deitrich Zimmer. Genetic identification could not be rigged, but the genetic print between close members of the same family was identical.

But it wasn't that simple. There was also the question of retina prints to be resolved. Yet, for someone ruthless enough to murder his own brother and skilled enough as a surgeon, that was easily rectified, just as it was for someone dedicated enough to sacrifice an eye.

It seemed clear that what Deitrich Zimmer had done was to have his own left eye surgically removed, then transplanted into the socket of his brother. His brother would have had to have been alive, of course, for the process to be done convincingly, and John Rourke did not want to consider the ramifications that that suggested.

But what had Deitrich Zimmer done to the baby he kidnapped?

Deitrich Zimmer had actually stolen two children, the newborn son of Lieutenant Martha Larrimore, born in the morning, and the newborn child Rourke's wife Sarah had delivered, probably only moments before Deitrich shot Sarah in the head.

Deitrich Zimmer kept the child of Martha Larrimore alive specifically for the purpose of killing it, to make everyone believe he had murdered the Rourke baby instead.

Then Zimmer arranged to fake his own death and that of Dodd; arranged for the abortive attempt at destroying the cryogenic chambers in which John Rourke and the rest of his family slept; arranged for the successful assassination of Akiro Kurinami, first elected president of Eden, and Akiro's wife, Elaine Halversen.

Then Dodd miraculously returned, claiming leadership of Eden, saying he himself was the victim of a neo-Nazi plot, exposing the body that was attributed to be his as that of a Nazi sympathizer in league with Deitrich Zimmer, who had

14

really died.

But, clearly, Deitrich Zimmer did not die.

What had he done to this man now called Martin, who was born of Sarah and himself? Rourke wondered.

Psychologists had perennially battled over the effects of environment versus heredity, but could the environment Deitrich Zimmer provided have wrought so much? Martin was clearly evil, not just misguided.

John Rourke reached for the helicopter's first aid kit in the same moment that Michael did. And he looked at his son.

Rourke considered himself luckier than most men. Michael was fine and good and strong, courageous. And Annie, his sister, was the epitome of all that was worthwhile in a woman — courageous, resourceful, loving. John Rourke had two children in whom he took great pride.

Chapter Three

They stood beside the skeleton of the helicopter that had brought them here. Still smoldering, it provided a modicum of needed warmth.

Annie was helping the women who had been rescued from the Land Pirates prepare for the arduous journey that lay ahead. The women now found themselves plunged into a survival situation more potentially deadly than their previous captivity. Natalia, perhaps suffering from a mild concussion but under the circumstances well enough to travel, kept an eye on Martin.

That she would use a gun, if necessary, to stop Martin from escaping was something John Rourke did not doubt for a moment.

Rourke's cigar was nearly burnt out now.

The cold was intense.

Michael and Paul, stripped down to ordinary pants and heavy sweaters, like John Rourke, had surrendered coats and snow pants to the women in an effort to prolong stamina and guard them against exposure.

When they presented their plan, John Rourke realized they had evidently worked this out in advance and were ganging up on him.

"This is potentially suicidal, Michael," John Rourke declared, watching his son's eyes.

"You got a better way of buying time, Dad?" Michael retorted bluntly.

"You can't do it, John," Paul declared. "You don't have much grey in your hair, but you've got enough. Michael now looks basically like you did when we first met on The Night Of The War. And that's exactly what Martin Zimmer looks like. That flesh wound Michael picked up in his left thigh is the only thing, and he figures he can fake his way around it."

"No, damnit," John Rourke told them both.

"At least hear me out, Dad," Michael said, still adamant. "If I can make them think Martin's been shot up a little and is all pissed off, they're not going to press by giving me some kind of identity quiz. As soon as they get me, give me medical attention and everything, I can order them to get me back to Eden so I can coordinate efforts to nail you guys . . . or something like that. I'll have to make it up as I go along. But I can convince them, make them believe I'm Martin. Once I reach Eden, I can slip away and meet you guys at the safe house."

There was a safe house, set up by Allied Intelligence, on the outskirts of Eden City. Just how safe it might prove to be was another question.

"The leg wound won't cut it; too many people saw you get hurt Michael."

"Exactly, but that'll work, Dad. Somebody shoots me in the leg again. Michael took one round, that's assuming anyone'll remember. Zimmer can have two bullet wounds. I tell them the aircraft crashed—they can see that with their own eyes—and that I stole a gun and took a couple of rounds before I was able to escape. With the helicopter gutted, I can tell them the fire started as soon as we hit the ground and that's how I was able to pull it off, in the confusion."

"You can't make them think you're Martin, Michael," John Rourke insisted.

"All I've gotta do is be surly, right? Somebody asks me something I can't answer, I complain about my leg hurting or the head wound, and tell whoever it is to shut up. That sounds like my brother." And he looked toward where Natalia kept Martin at gunpoint. "I can aim the search and destroy teams in another direction, buy you time. Otherwise, the best we can hope for is a standoff as soon as the Land Pirates and the Eden armed forces catch up with us, with us holding Martin while those women we freed die of exposure. What choice do we have, Dad?"

John Rourke looked at Michael, looked at him hard, then stared at Martin Zimmer, who was some distance away.

"I don't like it either, John, but it'll work," Paul said. "I don't like it a bit."

"If you can hold on to Martin," Michael said, "then you can use him as a bargaining chip with Deitrich Zimmer, maybe force Deitrich into operating on Mom to get that bullet out of her brain. That's why you want Martin. You're not going to kill him, no matter what he is, because he's your flesh and blood and Mom's flesh and blood, just like Annie and I are."

"You think you've got this whole thing psyched out," John Rourke said, nodding his head. "You . . . and you, Paul. Gang up on me, right?"

"It's logic, John."

John Rourke looked at Paul Rubenstein, then nodded his head. Without looking at his son, he said, "You'll need to swap clothes with Martin. We'll have to measure exactly where that first bullet went in in relationship to Martin's left trouser leg, so we can put a bullet hole there that will correspond. Then we'll have to smear some of the blood from the fresh wound onto the old hole."

"Natalia already said she'd fire the shot," Michael said.

"Ohh, you got her in on this, too, huh? Is Annie in on this thing as well?"

Paul looked away and Michael just smiled. . . .

His chest was bigger than Martin's. His biceps were also larger, and his triceps were better developed. And, when they exchanged clothes, he noticed something else: Martin was not circumcised. At the time that Michael Rourke was born, popular wisdom held that it was sound medical prac-

18

tice to circumcise all boys. So he had been circumcised.

Martin, of course, had warned him, "With that Jewish thing that they did to you — I have read about the practice, don't be fooled — the first time anyone sees you —"

"Well, tell me, brother Martin, you run around in the nude a lot in front of your soldiers? Didn't think you were that kind of a —"

"Laugh while you can, Michael. Laugh while you can."

Michael looked down at himself. The clothes were a decent enough fit, he supposed, but not to his liking. The trousers weren't too sturdy-looking. The shoes, rather than boots, expensive-looking but not too practical. And the shirt, which had little dots in the material, looked more like something a woman would wear. "You know, you may look like a Rourke, Martin, may have the same genes, the same blood, the whole thing, but do you know what a real Rourke would have done?"

Martin said nothing for a moment, then shrugged his shoulders as he buttoned on Michael's shirt. "No, what?"

"You don't want this impersonation to succeed, right? So you should have done something to make these clothes of yours unwearable." Michael grinned at him. "Here's a good Twentieth Century word for you, Martin — chump."

"What's a chump?"

"Somebody who acts stupid, Martin. Like you, buying all this Nazi garbage from Deitrich Zimmer. Why don't you —"

" — straighten out, Michael?" Martin asked, then laughed. "You and Dad and sister Annie and that disgusting Jew she's married to would —"

Michael Rourke took a step closer to Martin Zimmer. "Annie's husband is the best friend I have in the world. He's more of a brother to me than you'd ever be, asshole."

Michael grabbed up his sweater before Martin could put it on. Let Martin freeze. The sweater could help to keep one of the women a little warmer. Michael Rourke knew a bit more about Martin now, having listened a little more closely to how Martin talked. . . .

"I'll do it," Annie said to her.

"I am fine. My eye is steady, and so's my hand," Natalia declared.

Then Natalia looked at Michael. He was standing there, waiting, just a few feet from her. He started to laugh, saying, "This is great, just great."

"What's great?" Annie asked him.

Natalia just looked at him.

Michael Rourke said, "The girl I love and my sister. What are they doing? Arguing over which one of them is going to get to shoot me!"

Natalia closed her eyes, then opened them, took a deep breath, released it, and said, "Stand perfectly still, Michael." She inhaled again, releasing only part of the breath this time. Then she steadied the gun between her knees, her elbows pressed outward as she sat on the ground, her eyes almost level with where she was going to put the shot.

Her .380 caliber Walther was the lightest caliber of any of the guns they had. She cocked the hammer, then slowly started the trigger squeeze.

When the gun went off, her ears rang and Michael fell down into the snow.

Chapter Four

If the enemy didn't show up reasonably quickly, he would freeze to death, Michael Rourke decided.

He walked as best he could, to keep the blood circulating in his feet. But the two leg wounds, Natalia's shallower than the first, were hurting badly and walking was becoming increasingly more difficult for him. His head wound, unbandaged, ached. His father had examined it, pronouncing it superficial. But it didn't hurt less because of that.

Michael Rourke took some little consolation from the fact that if he died, until enemy medical personnel were able to take a retinal print and check his DNA, he might very well have everyone convinced that Martin had died instead. Unless someone who knew better noticed his circumcision. Such a deception, even in death, would slow up the search for his father, his sister, Natalia, and Paul. He'd considered that possibility before but had never mentioned it to anyone.

It had been hard enough as it was, getting his father to agree to this potentially suicidal charade.

He'd been talking to himself as he walked and waited, trying to think like Martin Zimmer and talk like Martin Zimmer. Fortunately, the former proved impossible, but he convinced himself he was really getting the hang of the latter. Martin's voice, essentially identical to his father's and his own, was just a little nasal, and he strung words together almost as if he had learned English as a second language, however well. Before his father and mother became so critically injured that their only hope for survival had been cryo-genic sleep, Michael had learned a good bit of German.

Natalia spoke it fluently and so had Maria Leuden, the girl with whom he'd slept, the girl he'd kept as his mistress but had realized he didn't love. And suddenly Michael Rourke stopped walking.

It was the first time he'd actually thought of Maria Leuden since awakening from cryogenic sleep, to discover that his mother was still deep in a coma but that his father, whose brain wave patterns had returned to normal, was be-ing awakened as well.

And, he realized now, one hundred twenty-five years later, Maria was dead and so were her children, if she'd had any.

His father had kept a considerable collection of books at The Retreat, some of them science fiction. Michael Rourke remembered reading one that was about a time traveller. The man had gone forward into the future, but everyone he had known and loved was long dead and gone when he got there.

Michael Rourke was luckier than that man.

Yet, he promised himself, someday, if he made it out of this, he would go to New Germany and find Maria's grave. And he would take Natalia with him. He would put flowers on Maria's grave. It hadn't been love. There was love with Madison, his wife who was killed so long ago. And there was love, even more intense, with Natalia. But he had cared for Maria Leuden. . . .

It consumed the better part of an hour for them to reach the height of the rift valley wall, and John Rourke had no way of knowing if, when they reached there, it would be ra-diation free. On both sides of the rift valley there were hot spots, which would remain hot for centuries to come. Any living thing that ventured there would die, sooner or later, as a result. But there was also a trail on this side, informa-tion about which Natalia and Annie had extracted—how, he didn't want to know—from Boris, the head of the slavers, whom they had kidnapped for the specific purpose of getting that information.

Parts of the trail, a secret route without risk of residual radiation hazard, came very close to the rift valley wall, while other parts were several miles to the west.

If they arrived at the height of the wall in a hot spot, they would have to go down again, continue along, then try the climb again. He would not put the women through it a second time unless he was sure, but time was against them and he'd taken the chance, a calculated risk he could confirm or deny with the radiation meter.

John Rourke left Annie, Natalia, and the twenty-four women about fifty feet below, and with Paul beside him, he took the climb. And, of course, he left Martin.

"You're worried about Michael. We're all worried about him, John." Paul clung to a spit of rock, his feet wedged against the rocky shale below it. Each time he moved, however slightly, some of the shale—about the consistency of fresh gravel—slipped.

"I know that," John Rourke almost whispered, testing the foothold he had before pushing himself up. "He's tough. He's got a good head on his shoulders. If anybody could pull it off, Michael could."

"Was he right? You plan to trade Martin?"

"If Deitrich Zimmer is too old to perform an operation on Sarah, if his hand isn't steady anymore, then he would have taught someone else his techniques, just in case he needed them or Martin needed them in order to stay alive."

"Suppose he saves Sarah's life? What then?"

John Rourke looked at his friend. "I'll keep my word and release Martin to him. And then I'll hunt them both down and kill them."

John Rourke kept climbing.

Chapter Five

"Martin? It's me, Gunther."

Michael Rourke looked at the face of the man who spoke. It was a plain face, the only feature that was re-remarkable — quite remarkable — being the eyes. They were a bright blue, a lighter shade than Natalia's but nearly as striking. And they were set with epicanthic folds.

The man was an officer in the Eden defense forces. The embroidered name tag on the parka he wore read "Hong."

"Gunther," Michael Rourke murmured, nodding. He made the first syllable of the man's name sound more like the word *goon* than the word *gun*.

Then Michael said nothing for a long moment, collecting his thoughts. The last thing he remembered was sitting down, because he was so tired and his legs hurt so badly from the gunshot wounds. The wounds were minor, superficial scratches, but there was still pain. That pain returned to him now, as did the full import of why he was looking up into this strange man's eyes.

Michael Rourke forced himself to sit up, the man named Gunther Hong and two other men, one an officer, one a senior noncom, assisting him. A fourth man, another senior noncom, brought blankets, laying one over Michael's lower body and wrapping the other around his shoulders and upper body. "What happened to you, Martin?"

Michael Rourke coughed, then cleared his throat, all of this unnecessary but calculated to plant an idea into the minds of these men. That idea was that if Martin's voice sounded just a little off, perhaps it was because he was coming down with something. Then Michael said, "There was a sudden storm. The Russian woman at the controls of the machine. She could not manage to land the thing properly. There was a fire. I grabbed a gun and jumped when we neared the ground. One of the bastards shot at me. I got these, damnit." Then he decided to try Martin's personality. "Did you think I was waiting out here, freezing to death, merely for the pure joy of it?"

"Well, no, but we—"

"Where were you?"

"We couldn't follow by aircraft and—"

"Help me up," Michael snapped.

"We have a stretcher, Martin," Gunther Hong volunteered.

"I will walk!" The men visibly recoiled from him for an instant, then started to help him stand. Feeling returned rapidly to the wounds in his legs, but his feet were numb and so were his hands. His head ached. He knew that was from the cold as well, his body rattling with the chill as a means of generating warmth. "I will need a doctor to tend to my injuries. We leave for Eden City at once. See to it," Michael ordered. "The swine escaped, but they cannot have gotten far. I want the search concentrated to the southeast. They will think we anticipate an attempt to reach their coconspirators in Eden. What they do not know is that I heard the younger of the two who look like me saying that they had transportation waiting to take them to the Gulf Coast. They will move east to escape the rift valley, then likely move directly south."

"Wouldn't they try to get to Eden? . . ."

25

"These men with my face. The older one of the two is John Thomas Rourke. He has survived for over six centuries, man! He has accomplished this by doing the unexpected. You have your orders. Now follow them!"

Michael no longer had to feign anger. The pain in his legs sparked the real thing with each step he took closer to the nearest of the massive battle machines. . . .

As Martin Zimmer, he was given the commander's cabin aboard the mobile fortress. The cabin was under no circumstances spacious, but it was more than adequate for one man. Rather than a bunk, the bed was a full-size one. And Michael Rourke leaned back into it now, his eyes closed as the Eden forces doctor, who seemed competent enough, tended his wounds.

Gunther Hong, whom Michael now realized was Martin's personal military advisor and held the rank of brigadier general, stood at the bedside. "You should take something, Martin. For the pain."

Taking something for pain might also loosen his tongue, and Michael Rourke couldn't risk that. "No. As soon as this is finished, I must get to Eden."

"We will be out of the rift valley and in one of the Safe Zones in twenty-seven minutes. There is a high-speed aircraft that will touch down at the same time. You will be in Eden in less than two hours, Martin. But why—"

"With John Rourke alive, there is no choice but to act at once."

"Perhaps I should contact the Herr Doctor, Martin."

Michael Rourke looked squarely at Gunther Hong. Did Hong mean Deitrich Zimmer? But there was no way to ask, and if he even seemed interested in the subject, that interest might betray him. Instead, he snapped at the doctor, who was cleaning the gunshot wound given him by Natalia. "Clumsy fool! You are causing me discomfort."

"I am sorry, sir, but—"

"Be done with this! I must reach Eden City and be able to act." He'd ordered that clothing be brought for him and hoped that it would also mean a weapon. The Eden origin assault rifle that was with Michael when they found him was nothing he could overtly attempt to hold on to, and his pistols had been left with his family.

Michael looked at the watch on his left wrist. It was Martin's watch, similar in size to his own Rolex but digital rather than analog. The case and the band seemed to be made of gold. Although it was obviously quite expensive, Michael preferred his own timepiece. Martin's watch showed eighteen minutes before the hour. By ten minutes after the hour, if the Eden war machine was punctual, he'd be airborne for Eden City.

The clothing arrived, military looking. And there was a pistol belt and a holster. Before Michael Rourke could say anything, Gunther Hong announced, "When we took up the chase, Martin, I ordered that some of your things be brought along."

"Good," Michael nodded. The doctor was finished patching up the gunshot wounds and had pronounced Michael's hands and feet were not frostbitten. Michael announced, "Doctor, out." Then he looked at Gunther Hong. "This thing with John Rourke and his son and the Russian woman and the others. I do not want John Rourke to become a rallying point for the dissidents of Eden. For that reason, once the rendezvous with the aircraft has been met, I wish for you to take personal charge in the field of efforts to capture or kill John Rourke."

"But, I—"

"You are loyal to me. This is known. You must obey these orders."

The blue eyes hardened, not with malice, but with something akin to pride. "Yes, Martin. If it is your will."

Michael Rourke nodded as, with some awkwardness,

he swung his bare legs over the side of the bed. "Bring me my things. I must prepare."

Gunther Hong complied, moving off quickly to the chair and returning with an armful of rather nondescript attire. There was a dark grey Nehru-style jacket, which he had first seen in videotape movies from the 1960's where people wore clothing variously referred to as "mod" or "kicky." A maroon turtleneck shirt, tight-looking blue trousers, and short black boots completed the outfit. There was a new set of underwear, too.

The dressings on his leg were waterproof, and there was time remaining. "I need to shower," Michael said.

"In here, Martin," Hong volunteered, pointing toward a small door off the side of the cabin.

Michael nodded, taking the clothing and starting toward the door.

Once inside the bathroom, he stripped away the remainder of Martin's things, urinated, then entered the shower stall. He washed his hair twice, soaking his body under the steaming water for a very long time. He was still chilled to the bone. On the plus side, his leg wounds were well bandaged and the cut on his head only bothered him when he touched it.

Senior officers of Eden lived well in the field, he concluded. The bathroom was far from Spartan.

If he ran out of time, it wasn't as if the aircraft would leave without him. He was, after all, Martin Zimmer. Michael Rourke smiled at the thought as he continued to enjoy the hot water. If he had to pick one person in the world not to be, it would be Martin Zimmer. Biological brother or not, the man was evil incarnate.

The key to Michael's success in the role, however, was to reach Eden City; then, with only a man or two with him, go someplace, anyplace. Lose, neutralize, or kill (if need be) the men and get away. The longer he hung around pretending to be Martin Zimmer, the greater his chances for being discovered.

Michael toweled dry, then started to dress. Martin Zimmer's trousers were a little loose at the waist and tight at the thighs, fashionable men of Eden evidently into underdeveloped muscles or looking as though their pants were about to rip. The trousers were also beltless. Except for a revolver on a Hip-Grip or the clip-type inside-the-waistband holsters, this made carrying a gun at the waist rather awkward. The turtleneck was somewhat tight as well, but satisfactory. He slipped into the high-collared jacket with no lapels. As long as he did not attempt to close the garment across his chest, it fit all right.

There was a hat that presumably went with the outfit. It was reminiscent of hats he'd seen worn by Mao Tse Tung in photographs. Michael Rourke looked at it in disgust, just carrying it in his hand instead of wearing it as he exited the bathroom.

"I have a gun for you, Martin," Gunther Hong said as Michael reentered the main portion of the cabin. Hong was holding a gunbelt in his outstretched right hand.

Michael Rourke didn't react instantly. The clothing he wore—Martin Zimmer's clothing—was obviously not designed for convenient concealment of a firearm. Nor did people travel openly armed in Eden City. As much as Michael Rourke wanted a gun, he was convinced Martin Zimmer would not have taken it. So he told Gunther Hong, "That is what I have the defense forces for, isn't it?"

But he'd be damned if he'd wear the hat.

They started from the borrowed cabin, toward the rendezvous with the aircraft, Michael presumed. As they moved through the bowels of the mobile fortress, men everywhere at their assigned tasks, Michael pondered something that had disturbed him from the very moment he first realized who Martin Zimmer was. Did Zimmer cultivate the near worship of John Rourke as some sort of evil joke?

29

There were statues everywhere in Eden, most particularly the one of his father — Martin's father, too — atop The Retreat. John Rourke's face was on the coinage, the stamps, even the health certificates. Why? And why did Martin Zimmer conceal his own face from all but a few?

Chapter Six

Snow fell heavily from a low, overcast grey sky. There was little wind. Each step was difficult, the terrain beneath their feet rocky and uneven, yet masked with more than a foot of reasonably fresh snow.

In the distance, to the east, the cloud cover was continually rent by chain lightning over the rift valley.

They were on the trail. That was pure luck, of course, intersecting the trail after the first climb, but a little luck — of the good kind — seemed long overdue them. Natalia and Annie stayed with twenty-three of the women rescued from the fortress of the Land Pirates. John Rourke and Paul Rubenstein carried the twenty-fourth woman, injured during the crash of the helicopter, between them on a litter.

This woman had the same chances for survival that the other women had. If shelter and food could be found soon, she would live. Otherwise, she would not.

To have used their radios to contact Allied Intelligence, assuming with all the electrical activity not far away in the rift valley the radios would have worked at all, would have been to invite capture by Eden forces and the Land Pirates.

The portion of the trail they followed led well west and, technically at least, was not part of Eden. Centuries ago, Before The Night Of The War, it had been known as Arkansas. Because of the starkness of the terrain, nothing looked familiar, and it was frequently necessary to check the compass and the map to make certain they did not stray from the trail.

No caves or large rock croppings presented themselves, so there was no place for shelter, not just from the cold but also from aerial observation. Because they were well enough away from the rift valley now, the Eden gunships could operate with impunity from the freak electrical storms.

John Rourke turned around as he heard Natalia calling to him, watching as she came forward with Annie and one of the freed women. She was very thin, with deep circles under dark, fearful eyes. The woman kept her head slightly down, the result being that her eyes did not meet John Rourke's as he looked at her.

Martin Zimmer stood between Natalia and Annie, an evil-looking smile on his face, his hands clasped on his upper arms, rubbing himself for warmth. "Why don't you just leave her, Dad?"

"Let's set the lady down," Rourke suggested to Paul Rubenstein, ignoring Martin's suggestion. Paul nodded as Annie and Natalia each helped in gently lowering the injured woman to the ground. Rourke dropped to one knee beside her, reassuring her, "We're only stopping to rest for a minute. You're doing fine."

She bit her lower lip as she forced a close facsimile of a smile.

John Rourke walked a few feet from her as Annie began to speak. "Daddy, we were talking back there, and Mary Ann—this is Mary Ann."

Again, John Rourke tried to meet the dark, furtive eyes of the woman, but she almost seemed intrigued with studying the toes of her worn cloth shoes instead.

32

"Tell them, Mary Ann," Natalia urged. "Tell them what you told us.

"I didn't mean to cause no trouble," the girl mumbled. John Rourke judged her age to be twenty, if that, but she seemed as careworn as a woman three times her age might be.

"It isn't causing trouble if you know something that will help us," Paul told her. He put his arm around Annie.

The girl did not speak.

John Rourke queried, "Is it something about where we are or—what?"

Her lips were cracked, the bottom one swollen a little as if she'd been struck. He'd noticed before the crash that many of the women kept by the Land Pirates for slavery and sex appeared physically abused beyond overwork and malnutrition. Mary Ann said, "My pa always tol' me to keep my mouth shut."

"I don't know about your father's motivation for that, Mary Ann," Rourke began, "but being silent is inappropriate under the circumstances. We're all in this together, and if you know something that will enable us to get out of this more easily, you should tell us. Do you understand?"

She was drawing in the dirt with her toes, swaying her body back and forth to some sort of unheard rhythm. But she nodded her head. Her fingers played with the tattered fabric of her dress. She didn't look up as she spoke. "I come from 'round here, mister."

John Rourke said nothing for a moment.

Mary Ann continued. "Over that ridge, I think. Ain't sure. Maybe's the town."

"Town," John Rourke repeated. He doubted her description of the place as an actual "town." Aerial photos he'd studied indicated isolated collections of buildings,

33

but there were no large human habitations within at least fifty miles of their current position. Still, if she were right, some small hamlet on the other side of the ridge might be possessed of a vehicle or even horses.

Even the smallest vehicle or a solitary horse would allow them to make contact with Allied Intelligence and get real help. There was a Resistance movement within Eden, of course, and there were personnel affiliated with it in the Wildlands as well.

"Let her take you to her little town. It will make you easier to find," Martin laughed.

Annie straight-armed Martin in the chest, knocking him onto his rear end in the snow. "Why don't you act like a human being?" she snapped.

John Rourke looked at Mary Ann. "Do you have people in your town? A family, I mean?"

"Uh-huh."

"Do you think somebody there might be able to loan us a vehicle or a horse? Just for a little while, Mary Ann?"

"Maybe."

"And your town is just over that ridge? Not much further than that?"

Mary Ann nodded.

John Rourke nodded.

Then he looked back toward the remainder of the women. The twenty-two all huddled together for warmth a few yards away would cover the distance that he judged to the ridge and over in perhaps a hard day's march. He could cover that distance much more quickly.

And he wondered about Mary Ann. . . .

His enormous body was resplendent with weapons, guns and knives. The uniform of the Land Pirates was no uniform at all. But this man, flanked by two other men of lesser height and bulk and not nearly so well-armed, was uniformed. He wore a coat with an enormous cape, which to Michael was reminiscent of Basil Rathbone's habitual attire as Sherlock Holmes in the video movies John Rourke had collected at The Retreat.

This man was obviously the leader of the Land Pirates.

The Retreat's video collection, which was temporarily unavailable to them, might best be described as eclectic. Michael Rourke's father had everything, from the profound to the frivolous, from science to drama to comedy. There were a number of the Sherlock Holmes films featuring Rathbone and Nigel Bruce. The giant Land Pirate further brought to mind the Sherlockian image because of the pipe he smoked, large bowled with a recurving stem. But, beyond the pipe and coat, nothing else was remotely civilized or gentlemanly. His overall appearance was otherwise closer to that of a dirty-looking grizzly bear. And the image of a bear was certainly more appropriate to his size.

The apparent leader of the Land Pirates was enormous.

"Elmo Babinski wants to apologize for what has happened, Martin. He says his men failed miserably."

That was the name supplied to them by Allied Intelligence. Michael quickly ran the few facts he possessed through his mind. Like the preponderance of the Land Pirates, although many were German and an almost equal number were of Second City Chinese extraction, Babinski was of Soviet origin, likely from the Underground City. Mentioning his name in the Wildlands supposedly struck terror in even the bravest heart, because Babinski, it was reported, seemed to enjoy cruelty.

Babinski stood now on the deck of the mobile fortress, his sheer bulk almost blocking the entrance to the waiting aircraft.

"His security sucked, and you know it," Michael told Gunther Hong. "Maybe I should tell him to kiss my ass."

"Martin! Remember, please, that we need his manpower. If you offend him now, I don't know—"

"Remember this," Michael told Hong in his best Martin Zimmer voice. "If he did not fear me, he would not be here." Michael increased his stride, Gunther Hong keeping up with him, until he stopped a few feet from Elmo Babinski and the two underlings. The wind that swept across the main deck of the fortress was bitterly cold, and whatever warmth he'd regained in the hot shower was long gone. "So." That was all Michael said, staring directly into Babinski's face.

Babinski's eyes were overly large and a muddy brown in color, and they went with the bear image very nicely. The eyes flickered, the stare wavering. "I came to say I'm damned sorry."

"You do not know how right you are," Michael nodded.

Babinski's body seemed to tense, and for a moment, Michael thought he had overplayed his hand. But then Babinski said, "Anyway, I'm sorry, Martin. We'll help your men get that dirty bastard Rourke and I'll bring you his fuckin' head on a stick if you want it."

"Fine. You do that. I am very cold and wish to board my aircraft. Good hunting." Michael started forward but Babinski did not move. Michael stopped and looked up at him. "Well?"

Babinski, his voice so low Michael could barely hear it above the keening of the wind, said, "I will kill John Rourke for you, Martin."

Michael said nothing. Babinski stepped aside. As Michael climbed the ramp toward the fuselage, he realized his fists were clenching.

Chapter Seven

Mary Ann would not walk abreast of them. And Natalia wondered if it were the girl's upbringing, or her period of slavery at the stronghold of the Land Pirates, or both, which made her so deferential to men.

Natalia walked beside John Rourke. They set a vigorous pace. Despite her emaciated appearance, the rescued girl, Mary Ann, was oddly enough able to match it. And Natalia reasoned that it might well be that the girl ran on some sort of mental ether, just because returning home to family and loved ones would soon be a reality.

The girl was out of earshot, in any event. Natalia Anastasia Tiemerovna had been at once waiting for and dreading the opportunity now presented to her. But she used it. "I need to talk with you, John."

"I always liked talking to you, and I suspect I always will. But there's nothing you have to say to me, okay?" He looked at her and smiled.

They had been walking for well over an hour, and as Natalia looked back, she could no longer even see the lightning over the rift valley. By now, Paul and Annie, along with Martin Zimmer and the other women, would be moving again, following them. John had made the right decision. Go on ahead, find transportation of some sort, see if transportation could be brought back for the women, or at the least bring clothing and food. While one of them did that, the other could go for help.

Natalia began to speak again. "Everyone thought—"

"Look—"

"Let me say it, damnit, John," Natalia almost whispered.

"All right."

"I was alone. You and Sarah were in the Sleep again. I never had any intention of taking the Sleep again myself. I told myself that maybe it was Fate or something. Can you imagine how awkward I felt? I was in love with you and you were in love with me and there was Sarah. You loved her and she became my friend? I mean, I was—There was just—"

John told her, "I understand. I approve—"

"Damnit, John! You approve? We didn't take the Sleep, Michael and I, so you could approve or disapprove. We took it so we could tell you. You would wake up sometime in the future and find out what happened to me and to Michael, and who knows what you would think. I owe you an explanation You do not owe me approval. I was lonely. Michael was there—"

"Look," John interrupted.

"No. You look, John. It's not that I attached myself to Michael because you were no longer around. Don't ever think that. I love you. But I love Michael. I did not realize that until after you were gone. And then I had a choice. I cannot be like you. I'm not that good. Maybe I'm too human. My life was meaningless. And there was Michael. And when he made love to me the first time—"

"I don't want to hear it, all right?" John said.

"No. You have to, so you will understand. I was afraid. I was terrified that I'd be telling myself it was you making love to me, like I had always wanted you to. But, when it happened, it was Michael. In reality and in my mind. I never gave myself to anyone like that before and—"

John stopped walking, his hands going to her arms,

turning her around abruptly to face him. "Look. Maybe you don't want my approval, but you're getting it anyway. I love you. I have since the first time I saw you. But it wouldn't work for us. Sure, if things had been different . . . but they weren't. We can still be friends. We can still have that kind of love. I'm happy for you and I'm happy for Michael. And maybe when Sarah awakens, comes out of it . . ." His words slowed, as if somehow they were recorded on a machine and the electricity were dropping off. "When she has that — that operation." He sniffed, and she saw tears forming in the corners of his eyes. "Maybe . . . maybe Sarah and I can just live like two — two — "

And he started to turn away from her. Natalia broke free of his hands, threw her arms around his neck, and drew his head down. He bent it toward her easily.

She held him.

Natalia knew the words he had been about to say. They were her dream, too.

The words he couldn't say without weeping were simple words, ordinary words. But they did not apply. She doubted they ever would to John and Sarah, to Paul and Annie, to Michael and herself, either.

Normal people were the words.

Normal people from the era in which they were born had all died one morning, except for those who were already dead or those who hid within the ground to die and raise another generation to die, and so on for centuries.

Normal people died. . . .

Michael Rourke listened.

Gunther Hong talked.

"We can turn this thing with Rourke to our advantage, Martin. You should see what the Herr Doctor thinks about it."

"How do you mean?" Michael asked noncommittally.

"Well, I mean, Babinski and his lieutenants know about Rourke, and of course the women taken from the Babinski's people. And I'm sure there are some others, but once he's taken care of . . . well—"

"Well?"

"Well, I mean, I don't see it as detracting at all from the messianic thing you and Dr. Zimmer are planning. I mean, anyone who has seen him will think he's seen you, except those few who know. And we can always liquidate Babinski. Like we talked about, if he becomes bothersome, we test a warhead out there. There'd be little to lose in country like that. Wait until the winds are right."

"Messiah," Michael Rourke repeated.

Gunther Hong laughed. "It is interesting, Martin. You've got to admit that. I mean, maybe this will push up the timetable a little bit, but, hey . . . He couldn't possibly realize it, of course, but John Rourke is almost helping you out. And the son, too. There's the body you need."

Michael didn't say anything.

He shifted in his seat to cover the effect of the chill, which ran along his spine.

Chapter Eight

Deitrich Zimmer's right eye moved over the computer screen.

On the hard disc, he had every bit of data that he felt was extant concerning the life of Dr. John Thomas Rourke. Like he himself, John Rourke's doctorate was in medicine. But Deitrich Zimmer doubted that their skills could at all be compared. In the Twentieth Century, when Rourke had learned the trade, medicine had been little better than sophisticated witch-doctoring.

And John Rourke had once been a case officer with the American Central Intelligence Agency. There was no telling how good Rourke was at that, but that he lived to leave the occupation at least said something for him. Rourke was a survivalist, prior to what was universally called The Night Of The War. He wrote and taught survival skills to military and police personnel around the globe. And he was a weapons expert.

Rourke was a peculiar man, his apparent tastes hardly describable as merely eclectic. The music in The Retreat ranged quite literally from Beethoven to the Beatles. One of the books Rourke liberated from The Retreat upon his return to the land of the living was Ayn Rand's *Atlas Shrugged*. The book was banned in Eden, of course. Martin should have pulled that copy as well.

Deitrich Zimmer had met John Rourke once, more than a century and a quarter ago. Their meeting had been very brief, taking place in a hospital corridor. And their meeting had been very violent. At the time, he had wanted John Rourke dead and thought that goal had been achieved. It turned out otherwise. Zimmer still wanted Rourke dead, and he would correct past errors in due course in order to achieve that goal now, one hundred twenty-five years later.

But in those intervening years, John Thomas Rourke had slept.

John Rourke had sustained injuries in that corridor, which had nearly claimed his life. Had it not been for cryogenic sleep, those injuries would have ended Rourke's life.

Cryogenic sleep's peculiar side effect, Zimmer himself discovered through his own experience, was physical rejuvenation. Even though cryogenic sleep was not some mythlike fountain of youth, which would have been wonderful, it did erase much of the toll of the years, strengthening the body and the mind to go on even stronger than before.

At the time of that encounter in the hospital corridor, a few moments before Martin was born to Sarah Rourke and Deitrich Zimmer shot her in the head, Zimmer had been thirty-four. He took cryogenic sleep twelve years later.

In those twelve years, Deitrich Zimmer had meticulously raised young Martin as his own son, his finest experiment. Escaping with the boy after killing the fortuitously available second infant, Deitrich Zimmer found asylum in a modest but adequate encampment that he had prepared as a last refuge. The site was in a remote portion of what was once known as Brazil.

With the assistance of several loyal Nazi comrades, he

accomplished the required genetic surgery to alter the Rourke child and make him his own.

The result proved to be all he had hoped it would, except for Albert Heimaccher's tendency toward petulance, which Martin unfortunately displayed. And, perhaps, that had been a characteristic of Adolph Hitler as well. Some accounts alluded to the trait.

The result was a boy he raised as Martin Zimmer, with the mental and physical capacities of John Thomas Rourke spliced to the genes of the greatest leader in human history, Adolph Hitler. Heimaccher, the source of the genetic material, was a direct descendant of the Führer through the Reichskinder program. After twelve years of intensive education utilizing the most dynamic techniques then available, it was time for them both to sleep.

The seeds of change were planted in Eden, and as Deitrich Zimmer had hoped, the intervening years allowed those seeds to take hold and flourish.

Deitrich Zimmer had awakened eighteen years ago. And he had awakened Martin Zimmer, his son now, in order to complete the boy's education and make him ready for power. Although Deitrich Zimmer's age was best calculated at sixty-four, according to comparative data, he was as fit as a healthy man of fifty. And this was adequate to his purpose as counselor to the new Hitler.

Cryogenic sleep not only rejuvenated the body, but in direct proportion to the duration of sleep, it prolonged the life span. Perhaps John Rourke suspected that.

Rourke slept five centuries between what was commonly called The Night Of The War and the period in which the great war between the Allies and the opposing Soviet culture was concluded. Then Rourke slept for another century and a quarter.

44

The effect of six hundred twenty-five years in cryogenic sleep on a human body such as Rourke seemed to possess could not be calculated. The computer model Deitrich Zimmer constructed indicated strongly that barring catastrophic illness or violent death, John Rourke would live well beyond the normal human life span, maintaining youthful vigor for a vastly extended period of time as well.

What if each year lost were a year gained? Zimmer's body shuddered with the thought.

And the same scenario, more or less, held for the rest of the Rourke Family.

And then there was Sarah Rourke, young Martin's mother.

Try as he had since his own return to life eighteen years ago, Deitrich Zimmer found himself unable to locate the cocoons in which the sleepers rested. But he knew there were two more. In one chamber slept Sarah Rourke, a bullet lodged deep within her brain. As long as John Rourke lived, Deitrich Zimmer wanted Sarah Rourke to live as well, but not a moment longer.

Because John Rourke had to know that the only man alive who possessed the surgical skills and techniques sufficient to remove the bullet was the man who had put it there. And that man could not be killed. To do so — for John Rourke to kill him — would be to sentence Sarah Rourke to sleep forever in something like death, perhaps even worse than death.

The remaining sleeping chamber held the odd man out.

Colonel Wolfgang Mann, field commander for the victorious Allied armies, was that man. Why had he abandoned the adulation of New Germany for the uncertainty of cryogenic sleep? Did he lust after one of the women? What was the answer?

But the survival of Wolfgang Mann provided an excellent opportunity for revenge. Mann, with the considerable aid of the Rourke Family, toppled the National Socialist regime of New Germany, and under Deiter Bern, there was established a democratic republic dedicated to stamping out forever National Socialism as the driving force of New Germany.

That form of government still endured in New Germany.

And Nazism in New Germany was all but extinct today.

That, too, would change.

Deitrich Zimmer glanced through the file. There was data concerning John Rourke's relationship with the Russian woman, Natalia Tiemerovna. But there was also data indicating that, while John Rourke had slept, in the relatively insignificant period of time before his Family joined him, the Russian woman and Rourke's son, Michael, became lovers.

As much as Zimmer would have wished, he did not consider it likely that he could use this development to drive a wedge between father and son. At best, they might hate each other privately but never question being allied against anyone perceived as their common enemy.

And there was Annie, the only daughter of John and Sarah Rourke, wife of the Jew Paul Rubenstein. From what Deitrich Zimmer had learned of her, she possessed many of her father's skills. And Annie Rubenstein had the peculiar ability that was referred to in the literature as Remote Viewing. Evidently, if the data was correct, she could see things that by all logic and reason she should not be able to see, through the use of her mind alone. If he could get her, he might experiment with her before killing her.

But her husband would die instantly, of course.

If there was an emotional link involved with her Remote Viewing capabilities, it might prove enriching to observe her reactions as Paul Rubenstein was killed.

There was a slowly growing Jewish population on the earth again. Deitrich Zimmer vowed to correct that. Some Jews had remained clandestinely practicing their faith in the Soviet Underground City in the Ural Mountains. Mid-Wake, the American citadel beneath the sea, had included Jews in its population as well.

Despite his being a Jew, Rubenstein was very clever, Deitrich Zimmer was perfectly willing to admit. But clever Jews died as surely as dull ones, Zimmer smiled to himself.

Clearly, when he succeeded in killing John Rourke, he would have to kill Michael Rourke and Natalia Tiemerovna and Annie and Paul Rubenstein at the same time.

Otherwise, the four surviving members of the Rourke Family would become even more formidable enemies than before.

There came a knock at the door of his laboratory. "Enter." It was Grundig, his general assistant. "Yes, Grundig, what is it?"

"Herr Doctor," she began, "there was a crisis, but it has been resolved."

"I am happy to hear that, Grundig. Its nature?"

Her eyes were wide behind her round rimmed glasses. "Your son—"

"Martin!"

"He is all right, Herr Doctor. The Rourke Family invaded the stronghold of the Land Pirates. Your son was kidnapped. . . ."

"He was—"

"He escaped. He returns even now to Eden City. He sustained no serious injury."

Deitrich Zimmer lit a cigarette.

Curiosity drove people beyond normal bounds.

So did revenge.

Deitrich Zimmer knew this from personal experience. Revenge and curiosity were his life force.

Chapter Nine

John Rourke was reminded of the collection of buildings in a muddy middle of nowhere that was the motion picture setting for Jack Schaefer's superb novel, *Shane*.

Mary Ann's home was not a town but rather an outpost of humanity. And barely that. A few buildings—seven in all—almost stared each other down across a wide, empty street that was like a gulf between them. Rather than mud there was snow, and although there were no vehicular tracks in the snow, there were hoofprints of shod horses.

"I see them," Natalia murmured, referring to the prints.

John Rourke stopped walking.

He stood about fifty yards from the nearest building. "Mary Ann?"

"Yeah?"

"Who lives here? A father and mother? A husband?"

"My old man.

Rourke caught Natalia's eye. Then he looked at Mary Ann again. "Is your old man your father or your husband?"

"My old man," she reiterated.

Natalia said, "I assume you'll go in from the front. Why don't I circle behind the buildings just in case?"

"Right," Rourke nodded. He touched Mary Ann's elbow and she started ahead, toward the wide street and the seven buildings. If her "old man" were neither father nor husband, then what was he?

John Rourke was already cold, but he removed the glove from his right hand as he started to walk, then the glove from his left. . . .

The German assault rifle she carried was reminiscent to her of the short M-16, the XM-77. The barrel of the German rifle was twelve inches in length, the buttstock collapsible. It fired a modern caseless rifle cartridge, but the overall dimensions were more submachine gunlike in proportion.

The stock of the rifle extended, Natalia Anastasia Tiemerovna moved along the scrub brush toward the rear faces of the four buildings on the north side of the street. As difficult as it was was for her to comprehend, the rear of the structures were even uglier than the front faces had appeared.

She was as close as she could get to the nearest of the buildings, which might be some sort of livery stable. There was a corral behind it, but no animals were in evidence.

Natalia started running, favoring the straight-line-is-the-shortest-distance-between-two-points theory rather than the zigzagging pattern. She had always been a fast runner, usually able to outlast and outdistance most of the men she'd known.

But Michael could outrun her.

She liked that.

And she thought of Michael Rourke now. She was in love with him, totally. At first that had frightened her, confused her. And she understood the almost slavish manner in which Michael's dead wife, Madison, had treated him, the same way his longtime mistress, Maria Leuden, had behaved. There was something about Michael that made a woman want to yield to him.

She was afraid for him now, afraid that the terrible risk he took pretending to be Martin Zimmer might cost him his life. And she was afraid for herself as well, because she would be desolate if he left her.

He was his father's son, but he was unique unto himself. Where John was reserved, Michael was wild. She realized that if she had somehow been John Rourke's lover Before the Night Of The War, he might have been like that. Both men had endured the terror and death, but Michael, unlike herself or John, was perfectly innocent of any of its cause.

And, perhaps that was the difference.

She reached the rear wall of the building. It definitely was a livery stable. There was smoke filtering through between the slats, likely from a cookstove or something similar, and with the smoke came the smell of manure.

There was an almost religious quality to the guilt she felt, which she knew John felt, too. To a lesser degree, Paul also felt it. Unlike Annie and Michael, who were children of The Night Of The War, she and John had been part of the opposing forces that had brought the war about. And Paul, although not in what was euphemistically called "the game" by some, was on the sidelines, as was every adult in the world. If one didn't try to prevent the unthinkable from occurring, then one was part of the reason that it did occur.

If she and John were guilty by sins of commission, then Paul felt himself guilty by sins of omission.

In this world, there were only four people who could have that guilt, and one of those was Sarah Rourke.

If John was right and there was a God, then why was Sarah Rourke on the edge of death?

Natalia closed her eyes for an instant, then opened them sniffing back a tear.

Michael had made her feel alive again, and she did not want to lose him, lose that. . . .

Michael Rourke cursed his lack of formal education. He knew so little about computers, beyond the comparatively simple machine at The Retreat, that he could do no more than turn on Martin Zimmer's unit. He could not access any of the files.

"Damnit," he muttered under his breath.

Inside that computer would almost certainly be information concerning Dr. Deitrich Zimmer. And Deitrich Zimmer could well hold Michael's mother's life in his hands.

Michael Rourke left the desk with its computer console and walked along the near wall of Martin Zimmer's almost ridiculously spacious office.

The only thing that pointed to Zimmer's Nazi leanings was a small brass globe—or maybe it was gold—which was placed on a shelf in the large bookcase before which Michael Rourke now stood. Atop the globe was a small, almost meticulously delicate swastika. . . .

The building at the near end of the four structures was a livery stable.

The building beside it seemed to be some sort of public house.

Mary Ann, bolder up until now, cowered by the low, wide doorway.

"What's the matter?"

"My old man'll be in there."

"Don't you want to see him?"

"Yeah, but—"

The unfinished sentence hung there in the air between them. And John Rourke suddenly understood. Sarah or Annie or Natalia would have read the reaction an instant sooner, he realized. She was afraid of her old man . . . that somehow he would punish her for being gone.

John Rourke turned the knob on the cast-iron handle of the door and opened it.

The unmistakable smells of marijuana and green beer assailed his nostrils, mingling on the cold air with the animal odors from the stable next door.

John Rourke went through the doorway first. . . .

Michael Rourke walked along the corridor of the capitol building's first floor, toward the staircase at its far end. Gunther Hong walked beside him. "I will show you, Martin, where our search teams are. The transponder signals on the situation map indicate the Rourke Family must be boxed in. We were able to field an SS Search and Destroy Team. I thought they needed the practice."

"Wise decision," Michael nodded, saying nothing else.

Instead of getting away, he was going deeper into Martin Zimmer's seat of government. The building itself reminded him of hazy childhood memories and photographs he had seen of classic small town courthouses.

They reached the staircase and started downward. . . .

Natalia Tiemerovna stopped moving when she heard the low growl from behind her. Her mind raced. The Germans had maintained a controlled population of dogs a century ago. There was no reason to suppose . . . she

53

turned her head very slowly. The Chinese of the Second City had kept wolves.

Mouth dripping saliva from bared fangs, hind legs flexed, a descendant, presumably, of one of those wolves stood behind her.

Chapter Ten

"Paul, they're too tired to go on."

"I know," Paul Rubenstein told his wife. Then he looked at Martin Zimmer's face. Martin was obviously cold and otherwise uncomfortable. But he was laughing. "You keep laughing, buddy, you won't have to worry about your father or your brother looking like you anymore. They'll have faces and teeth."

Martin Zimmer's smile disappeared.

Annie said, "I'll get them together."

"Don't let any of them get too comfortable," Paul advised. "We might have to move out fast."

The configuration of the terrain here was unrelieved flatness. If they were spotted from the air or pursued by a fast vehicle, there would be no place to hide and it would be a standoff at best, with Martin Zimmer as the sole bargaining chip. And to produce him might be sealing Michael's death.

But the women were exhausted.

"Bring her over here. Come on," Paul ordered, Zimmer not even nodding, but turning toward the gathering knot of twenty-two freed women, the twenty-third one on the litter he and Martin carried between them. . . .

The map of the Wildlands dominated an entire wall.

But it was only a computer screen. As Michael watched, he was able to discern the exact positions of the ground patrols sent out, he had hoped erroneously, after his family." But one of the patrols was far from the others, on the western side of the rift valley.

"That is the SS?"

"Yes, Martin."

"Why are they covering the wrong side of the valley?"

"It was only thought to be good sense, in case the Rourke Family attempted to trick us all by fleeing in the opposite direction."

"And why would a man as clever as John Rourke do something like that?" Michael pressed. If he pressed too hard, or should try to order the withdrawal of the search and destroy team, he might only be signing his family's death warrants, and his own as well.

"Well?"

Gunther Hong shrugged his skinny shoulders. "I can recall them if you wish, Martin."

Michael Rourke looked at the map position. "How many men in all?"

"Fifteen — twelve SS and three Land Pirates."

"The scum. No. Let them waste their time, then." Michael Rourke prayed they would be doing just that. . . .

Natalia had several possible solutions to her immediate dilemma. She merely had to fire a gun and kill the creature. But if she did so with an ordinary gun, the shot or shots would be heard by anyone who might be inside the building behind which she now stood statuelike, or inside the livery stable, or for that matter anywhere within the seven-building town. Even using her PPK/S with the suppressor would elicit yelps of pain from the animal. The same could be said if she used her knife. "Shit," Natalia said out loud.

There was nothing to do but wait, and hope the wolf did the same. . . .

John Rourke held open the door just long enough for the terrified Mary Ann to follow him inside. Because of their natural light sensitivity, his eyes adjusted quickly to the darkness within. A crude lamp burned on either side of a large room, with rough-hewn wooden clapboard walls and erratically spaced support posts running between floor and ceiling. There was a fire burning in the stone hearth that dominated the far wall, and a cast-iron stove, black as night, was at the center of the room. Along the wall to his right was a bar of sorts, just a long table with a few men leaning against it, a few glasses near them and a few bottles of mixed sizes on a narrow counter behind it.

There were several tables scattered indiscriminately about the room, a few more men sitting in small groups at two of them.

Several of the men looked toward the doorway as John Rourke said, "I have a girl named Mary Ann with me. She's related to somebody around here."

"Related! Related? Ha!"

John Rourke looked toward the bar. One of the men leaning against it had spoken. He wore several layers of ragged clothing, all of it appearing filthy. Rourke noticed the butt of a pistol—at the distance it looked like a Beretta 92F—thrusting up from the waistband of baggy trousers, which were bound together with a length of frayed rope that looked nearly black.

"Ivan's my old man, mister. We ain't related none."

Rourke didn't look at Mary Ann as she spoke, but he nodded that he heard her.

"There be Ivan."

Her right hand passed the edge of Rourke's peripheral

vision and his eyes followed in the direction she pointed. A big man but young, sitting at one of the tables with two other men, seemed to be her old man, Ivan.

"My friends and I found Mary Ann a prisoner of the Land Pirates. My name's John Rourke."

Ivan spoke. "And I'm fuckin' George Washington. Yes'erday I was Lenin and t'morrow I'm gonna be Lady Godiva!' And he laughed, and the armed man at the bar—they were all probably armed—laughed, then some of the others joined in.

John Rourke stood where he was, saying nothing.

The laughter abruptly stopped when Ivan snapped, "Get yo ass ove here, bitch!" Mary Ann scurried across the room to him, dropped to her knees at his feet, and made to put her head on his thigh. He kicked her away. She fell, sprawling onto the hard-packed dirt that comprised the floor. Ivan stood up. He was one of the largest human beings John Rourke had ever seen. "Them's nicelookin' guns yo got. Gimme 'em and maybe yo'll walk outa here."

John Rourke was taking a slow step left so the door wouldn't be directly behind him, but there would be a solid wall instead. "We're being pursued by the Eden Armed Forces and the Land Pirates. We have a lot of people in need of shelter from the cold. I need to borrow a horse, unless you've got a vehicle that runs."

"They's a lot o' us. Jes' one o' you. Gimme 'em guns."

"Give 'em to 'im, hear!" This time it was the dirty man lounging beside the bar who spoke.

There were ten men, counting the bartender. Allied Intelligence indicated that these subminiature towns were occasionally nothing more than a den of thieves and killers. The usual armament was material scavenged from the battlefields following the conclusion of hostilities with the Soviets over a century ago, along with some old weapons from the original Eden stores, which dated back five centuries before that.

The Beretta worn by the man at the bar was one such item, the military pistol of the preWar United States armed forces. And John Rourke smiled as he thought of it. Before The Night Of The War, he'd known innumerable people in the firearms trade, Beretta personnel among them. They would have been proud to know that six centuries after manufacture their products were still in use. Michael himself carried two of them.

John Rourke's own guns were more than six centuries old, too.

And he had no intention of parting with them. He told Ivan and the others, "I didn't come here for trouble. I am John Rourke, but your acceptance of that as fact is immaterial at the moment. As to my guns, . . . well, all you'll get of them is the lead part. So, let it alone and tell me how I can get hold of a horse." And then he looked at Ivan. "And treat the woman decently."

Ivan spit toward her and Mary Ann recoiled, as if from the bite of a snake.

"You boys all spread out, hear?" Ivan ordered. The men in the bar, some of them already standing, started to move.

John Rourke didn't budge.

There were more scavenged weapons, some things that even looked homemade. During the Twentieth Century, a substantial and highly vocal minority had fought unceasingly for what they called "gun control," really people control instead. Chief among their spurious arguments was that by some mystical method the denial of availability of firearms to the law-abiding would prevent criminal misuse. A handmade shotgun or zipgun, made from pipe or radio antenna or other available materials, was as deadly as the finest weapon ever made. And anyone could make one, even churls such as these. Guns were never a problem, just a relatively minuscule

59

percentage of the people who used them.

The bartender had an assault rifle, a wartime AKM-96 of the sort the Russians had used in their fight against Mid-Wake.

John Rourke hadn't done this sort of thing since that war, when he'd measured his reflex time against equipment in New Germany shortly after this. Awakening, he discovered that his time was slightly better than it had been before.

"I still need transportation. I'll get it. It's your decision if all or any of you are alive at that time."

"Fuck off!" Ivan shouted back.

John Rourke shook his head. "How sad it is that what little of the English language remaining to you has devolved to this."

"What the hell he say?" It was the man at the bar.

"Let's do it, then," John Rourke urged, not desirous of wasting any more time than he had to here.

Ivan started to draw.

John Rourke saw the muscles in Ivan's face and neck and around his eyes flex in the split second before the hand moved. So Rourke's hands were already in motion, the two stainless steel Scoremasters filling his fists and out of his belt, muzzles punching forward, the hammers cocking under his thumbs. The first fingers twitched and the pistols bucked lightly. There was a simultaneous double roar that made his ears ring, and already the guns were firing again.

And Ivan was falling down dead, his eyes wide open in startlement evolving to death, a wartime German service weapon falling from his fingers.

The laughing man at the bar fell in the same instant, his Beretta flying from his hand.

The bartender with the assault rifle slammed back into his motley array of bottles, the rifle discharging into the bar itself, bullets hitting the laughing man

60

in the back, flinging his body forward.

The two men flanking Ivan—one had a homemade pipe shotgun already in his hands and the other was struggling with something inside his clothing that looked like a zipgun—went down, the one with the zipgun jack-knifing first, then sprawling sideways over the rising muzzle of a gun in the hands of a man from the next nearest table.

But John Rourke shot him as well.

Someone shouted, "Wait up!" There were three men running for the front door and Rourke let them go.

The last man in the room dove behind his table, and with the Scoremaster in his right hand, Rourke lobbed a solitary round toward him. It was nearly empty, anyway.

Rourke thumbed up the safety, stepping back and left as the man behind the table punched a German service pistol toward him and fired. The man missed, as Rourke had at once anticipated and hoped.

The Metalife Custom 629 Smith was in Rourke's right hand now. He double actioned it once, the 180-grain jacketed hollow point exiting the .44 Magnum's six-inch barrel and zipping through the table, into the man. The man's body slammed back into the hearth, his clothing catching fire as he fell.

John Rourke logged another shot inside the man's head which was unaccountable.

Rourke turned halfway toward the front doorway, just in case the three men who had fled returned.

Mary Ann knelt speechless beside Ivan's body, hands clasped over her ears, tears streaming down her dirty cheeks.

He moved toward the last man he'd shot, kicking the body over onto the back to extinguish the flames.

There was a small back door at the far end of the bar which Rourke had noticed earlier. And it opened now.

Natalia came through the doorway, her assault rifle in her hands.

"You fire a shot?" Rourke asked her.

"Wolves around here. I had to kill one."

"Me, too," John Rourke told her.

Chapter Eleven

Gunther Hong started the interactive digitized display into motion, stopping it occasionally to make a comment, using a light pen to manipulate images.

It was a map of the western hemisphere, its easternmost point the Brazilian coastal reentrant into the South Atlantic, its westernmost point the Hawaiian Islands.

There were targets marked on the map.

Michael Rourke recognized most of them. And he presumed Martin Zimmer would recognize all of them. The charade was wearing thin, but to attempt to leave during Gunther Hong's briefing to the staff—officers, both Eden Forces and Nazi (although not uniformed), and some civilians as well—would be a dead giveaway. The Nazis were obvious, however, both by the swastika-emblazoned party pins in the collars of their turtleneck sweaters and their undeniable military bearing.

The intelligence data Michael could collect here might prove invaluable.

"The one problem area," Hong said, halting the display and working some knobs on the control panel, "is here." The Hawaiian Islands expanded across the screen, filling it. The light pen touched at Oahu, over New Honolulu. "The United States Fleet. Mid-Wake, as we know, was able to utilize the basic Soviet submarine designs of better than a hundred years ago and improve upon them. The resultant craft are capable of high-speed underwater and surface navigation, with aircraft and missile launching capabilities. Some of those missiles have recently been armed with nuclear warheads. We have to knock out Pearl Harbor totally before we strike at our other targets."

Michael Rourke didn't know whether to laugh or to cry. If Admiral Yamamoto had suddenly walked into the underground briefing complex, Michael wouldn't have been surprised.

Hong went on. "Pearl Harbor is on low-level alert status and has been for several months. Which means, of course, they'll be a little sloppy about it by now. Before we strike, we intend to soften them up a little. Gruppenführer Croenberg will fill us in from here."

Croenberg. In the first instant Michael entered the room beside Gunther Hong, his eyes were drawn to the man. Croenberg somehow seemed to exude intelligence, discipline, competence—and evil.

Bowing slightly toward Michael as he stood, Croenberg began to speak. "To recap, gentlemen, the National Socialist movement has placed agents in key positions within the Hawaiian chain over the last two years. Our agents report that they are ready to undertake their assigned tasks when the order is given for them to do so."

Croenberg extended his hand toward Hong, receiving the light pen and nodding curtly in return. With the light pen moving over the console's monitor, its motions repeated on the screen which filled a third of the area of the far wall, he pointed to various locations one after the other. "At the designated moment, such acts of sabotage will be committed as to produce long-term disruption of power and communications facilities, defense sensing and imaging installations, etc. And, of course, once our agents are away, preset bio charges will detonate. The result should be temporary decapacitation of nearly ninety per cent of the island's population, including those military personnel not operating within a hermetically sealed environment.

"Controlled EMPs will be executed over Pearl Harbor itself," Croenberg went on, clearing his throat. And "EMP," Michael knew, was an Electromagnetic Pulse, derived from a nuclear explosion. "We will be utilizing low-yield devices, of course. Specially trained and equipped SS units will then depart Staging Area Alpha, here on Molokai. . . ." The image shifted on the screen so rapidly that watching it was almost nausea inducing. "They will seize control of their respective areas, and barring the unforeseen, Pearl Harbor and an estimated sixty-seven percent of the American naval fleet will be under our complete control.

"Those vessels affected by the EMPs — ones well out to sea, I should add — will be powerless to resist once our forces are in place. Only vessels in deep water will be operational, and that will comprise a minuscule percentage of the whole. Individual commanders refusing to surrender could be neutralized easily."

There was silence, and everyone looked at him. Michael Rourke realized it was suddenly incumbent upon him to speak. But the slightest error could cost him his life. Carefully, he composed and asked his question. "The likelihood of having to neutralize these independent commands, what is it?"

Croenberg seemed satisfied. "The Americans are strong-willed. Our best estimates are that more than ninety percent of those who were operational would resist, either by attempting to launch a counterattack on their own initiative or by fleeing to Mid-Wake."

Michael Rourke merely nodded. . . .

Paul Rubenstein climbed the only high outcropping of rock within sight. Doing so got him some twenty feet above the plain. Using a pair of German field glasses, he looked first toward the rift valley.

Along the horizon line to the east, he saw no spotter or attack aircraft. But, as he intensified his focus and turned his glasses to the south, he saw a snow trail, the sort that would be made by a vehicle moving at reasonably good speed. He watched it for almost a minute. Its vector was taking whatever made it straight toward their position.

Paul Rubenstein cased the field glasses and, carefully lest he slip on the rock face, started down.

They would have to move—and quickly, too. . . .

Mary Ann was still sobbing. She had called him a murderer.

If he lived to be a thousand years old, John Rourke would never understand why or how a woman could love someone who treated her with such obvious contempt. And, apparently, Mary Ann had loved her "old man" very much.

When the three of them entered the stable, they found a dozen horses and an equal number of crude saddles and attendant tack.

Natalia suggested, "Why don't we do as planned, John? One of us goes for help, while the other takes the rest of the horses back for Annie and Paul?"

John Rourke nodded. "There aren't enough horses anyway, so the loss of one more won't matter. You link up with Hilda, Dan, and Margie. Take a spare animal with you just in case—"

"John, you're better on horseback than I could ever be. And you're going to tell me I'm lighter, so the horse won't tire as easily. But you're still better, which makes your reaching help much more reliable a proposition."

John Rourke looked at her and smiled. "If there were ever a person with the power of logical persuasion, it's you. Fine. What do we do with Mary Ann? Can't leave her here for those other three or whoever else is around to come back and harm her."

"I'll take her with me."

John Rourke nodded, starting across the stable floor and looking into each of the crudely carpentered stalls. None of the animals was outstanding, all of them seeming malnourished and mistreated. But the largest of the animals—about fifteen hands—seemed satisfactory. He was a grey, and John Rourke was partial to that color in an animal. But he looked to be the strongest of the horses as well. "I'll take him and one other." The grey was a gelding. "That mare," Rourke decided, pointing to a smaller-statured bay who looked like she might be a good runner. "And I'll take the best saddle."

There wasn't much to choose from in that regard, all of the saddles basically crude seats and nothing more. They were most reminiscent of poorly crafted copies of the saddles the German Long Range Mountain Patrols of a century-ago utilized, similar in design to the old United States Cavalry McClellans.

With what appeared to be the most solid of the saddles selected, John Rourke set it aside, then began saddling the other animals that Natalia would be taking back to Annie and Paul and the women. There were not enough horses for everyone to mount, but resourceful use would still be of aid to the group.

And he looked at Mary Ann, standing in the middle of the stable floor, still weeping. . . .

John Thomas Rourke had the stirrups lengthened as much as he could, but they still weren't comfortable. His knees higher than he liked them, he swung his mount and looked back along the street running between the seven buildings of the unnamed town. There was not the time

67

to bury Mary Ann's "old man", or any of the others. Those of their weapons that might prove even modestly serviceable were with Natalia and Mary Ann now, the others sufficiently dismantled as to be inoperable.

The three men who had run still worried him a little, but there was no time to do anything about them. Holding the reins for the second animal, John Rourke dug in his heels to the grey, urging the beast ahead to the north. . . .

The injured woman on a litter between Paul and Martin Zimmer, Annie Rourke Rubenstein urged the twenty-two other women onward. "If you don't hurry, they'll catch up with us and some of you could be killed, and the rest of you will be returned to the Land Pirates. Hurry!" She felt like someone's mother, warning a poorly behaving child to be good lest the bogeyman come.

One of the women called back to her, saying, "We was better off with them, the Land Pirates."

Annie didn't know what to say in reply.

Chapter Twelve

Martin Zimmer's balcony looked out from Eden City's highest tower, over the city itself and the vast expanse of Georgia that lay toward the north.

The atmosphere was richer now than it had been a century and a quarter ago, largely due, of course, to German-led efforts in regreening the South American rain forest lands. And, although the population of the earth had doubled and redoubled many times over, there was still comparatively little industry and the air was very clean.

The result was, as the sun began to set, that Michael Rourke could see so far into the distance he could almost fantasize seeing the mountain where The Retreat, the only home he had ever really known, was located.

He knew that was physically impossible, however.

But a thought of home, even though that home was now a museum controlled by enemy forces who wished to kill him and his entire family, was still of comfort, however ephemeral. And he thought, specifically, of Natalia. His father had taken the news of his and Natalia's liaison so well it was almost scary. But his father was, after all, John Rourke. Natalia. To lose Natalia was something of such import Michael Rourke could not comprehend it, nor did he try. Perhaps John Rourke had never thought of Natalia in that way, never considered her "his woman," therefore . . . therefore, what?

Michael Rourke missed Natalia more than he could ever have thought possible after the death of his wife, Madison.

And he would never see Natalia or anyone he loved again if he did not get out of here.

Michael assessed the situation. He was still being viewed as Martin Zimmer. That would not last. He had the uncomfortable feeling that Croenberg, the SS major general, already saw through him.

If Deitrich Zimmer were to suddenly arrive, that would be it.

To get away from the building, he could overpower a guard and steal a gun, or he could just walk out. After all, as Martin Zimmer, it was his building to command, as were the guards. And the information he had in his head concerning the impending attack on Pearl Harbor as a prelude to war was vital. That information had to be transmitted to Allied Intelligence so the attack could be foiled and, hopefully, the war forestalled.

Michael Rourke had the uncomfortable feeling that history was repeating itself, but at a much accelerated pace. A World War II-like beginning to what might be World War Last . . . .

James Darkwood walked alone along the street, the buildings surrounding him like towering mountain pinnacles. He had been born in Mid-Wake, raised and schooled in the Hawaiian Islands, only returning to Mid-Wake for the Naval Academy and his specialized Naval Intelligence training.

A place like Eden, now the oldest surface city on Earth, still amazed him. There were a comparative few tall buildings in New Honolulu, but not this obsession for a terrestrially bound aggregation of synth-concrete slabs to reach into the sky.

He thrust his hands into his jacket pockets. He was alert to any sounds in the gathering darkness that might be at all out of the ordinary. His face was not known here in Eden City, nor was there any reason to suppose that anyone might take even the briefest second look at him, but he was still operating in enemy territory.

There was considerable pressure exerted, even at the Naval Academy, for him to enter the submarine service. He was even offered a berth aboard the new *Reagan*.

The United States Nuclear Submarine *Ronald Wilson Reagan*, Jason Darkwood's ship, was the most decorated vessel of the Mid-Wake fleet. There were two submarines to bear the ship's name in the intervening one hundred twenty-five years, none of them (because it was peace-time) approaching her glorious record.

This latest vessel, James Darkwood feared, might have the chance to prove herself . . . and quite soon.

She was, officially, a "Submersible Carrier Vessel Navy," an aircraft carrier with the ability to operate above or below the surface, like a spacecraft of the ocean, enormous, fast, and deadly if need be.

If he ever became anything but a landlocked sailor, he'd love to serve aboard her.

But uniformed duty was a luxury he could not afford now. The importance of on-the-ground intelligence gathering in these dark days could not be measured. And, although he was only a small part of a large operation, each fragment of information acquired had the potential to be a breakthrough.

War was coming.

If the when and where of it could be determined, its toll might be less telling.

71

As he rounded the corner, he saw a tall, almost impossibly long-legged silhouette against the lights of the early evening traffic. It belonged to Manfred Kohl, his partner for the last two years.

"James," the figure said, stepping back into the shadows.

"Manfred," Darkwood nodded. Kohl lit a cigarette, the downturned corners of his mouth and the worried look in his eyes visible for the briefest instant in the momentary flaring of his lighter. "So?"

"Martin's in there. Has to be. I saw the usual motorcycle escorts, everything. Went in through the underground garage. That means our friends did not make it."

"You're jumping to conclusions, Manfred." James Darkwood lit his own cigarette. The lighter was an original Zippo, identical to the one John Rourke carried, a gift from Rourke to Darkwood. Jason Darkwood was a non-smoker, but according to stories told concerning him, he had a genuine fondness for antiques. Aside from John Rourke's, James Darkwood had only seen two similar lighters in his entire life. This one was solid brass, marked "1932 ZIPPO 1987" at its base. It was probably worth more than the Steinmetz James Darkwood wore on his left wrist.

Darkwood inhaled the smoke of the cigarette deep into his lungs.

Kohl said, "Why am I jumping to conclusions, James?"

Darkwood exhaled, saying, "Well, for one thing, we've never been able to tell for certain that those motorcycle escorts really are for Martin. And we don't know what Martin looks like. Only a handful of his people do. And, even if Martin did come back, that doesn't mean the Rourke Family failed in its mission or got caught. It only means Martin wasn't there. Maybe. You're a worrier, pal."

72

Kohl's shoulder shrug was just visible in the shadows. "Perhaps."

Darkwood looked at the orange glowing tip of his cigarette. A lot of people smoked these days. The Germans had developed non-carcinogenic tobacco more than a century and a half ago, and in the last fifty years or so, the habit had caught on again. It was still possible to smoke to excess and cause other sorts of damage to the body, but the moderate smoker who kept to something like a pack or so a day could smoke all his life without any fear of physical repercussions. Synthetic nicotine provided taste satisfaction, but there was no chance of nicotine addiction.

The only person alive who'd smoked the real things regularly more than six centuries ago was Major Tiemerovna. She smoked these now and approved of the taste.

He watched the building. It was the tallest in Eden City.

From the outside, no one would have suspected it was the actual seat of government. The capitol, two blocks away, was a quaint structure, centuries old in appearance. Few persons knew that a tunnel, traversed only by high-speed battery-powered cars, connected the two structures.

He agreed with Manfred Kohl. The motorcycle escorts seen from time to time had to be for Martin.

And maybe something had gone wrong for the Rourkes.

Chapter Thirteen

Tall, lean, shaven head, the skin so tight over his skull that the veins could be seen pulsing, Croenberg stood in the doorway, right hand in the pocket of his jacket. Michael Rourke looked at him for an instant longer, then asked, "What is it?"

"I had hoped that I could speak with you, Martin."

"I am tired. As you know, I started the day rather poorly."

"It will only take a moment." Croenberg smiled. Michael Rourke didn't like the smile because it reminded him of a death mask.

"All right." Michael stepped aside and Croenberg walked inside. The door closed and Michael was alone with him. Gunther Hong was, presumably, following orders and actually taking to the field to assist in the search for the Rourke Family, which Michael prayed would be abortive. Michael had dismissed the uniformed manservant shortly after Hong left, needing to be alone . . . or as alone as he could be.

Croenberg crossed the room, unbidden, and stopped just inside the balcony doors. "The view from here is incredible."

"I suppose," Michael responded, trying to sound as though he saw that same view every day. But it was incredible. Dark now, the city of Eden was alive with lights, which sparkled like jewels in the darkness.

And Croenberg turned around, his hand out of his pocket and a gun about the size of Natalia's Walther PPK/S pointing directly at Michael's center of mass. "Who are you?"

Michael looked away from the solitary orifice of the gun and into the two orifices that were Croenberg's deep-set grey-blue eyes. "I could have you killed for this."

Croenberg then blew the whole thing. He began speaking in German, Michael recognizing just enough of it to realize the vocabulary was too much for him, the speed too rapid. Croenberg continued speaking. Michael sat down in one of the overstuffed leather chairs, opening the lid of the cigarette box, then using the battery-powered table lighter to fire the cigarette he placed between his lips. Whether Martin smoked or not was academic. Michael did, occasionally, and the game was up; so now seemed like the ideal time.

Croenberg continued speaking in machine-gun-rapid German. Michael exhaled smoke through his nostrils, smiled, and asked, "Are you anywhere near being through, Croenberg?"

Croenberg laughed, the laughter quite genuine in nature. "You really look like him, you know? Are you John Rourke?"

"You flatter me," Michael said with a wave of his hand, which held the cigarette, and a smile. "I'm Michael Rourke, John Rourke's other son. I'm five hundred years older than my brother Martin, but still, there's a marvelous resemblance."

"You are very bold, and intelligent, too, I think. Since these remarks will never leave this room, I will speak freely. More intelligent, I think, than your 'younger' brother . . . hmm?"

"Nice of you to notice."

"Where is he?"

75

"Are you trying to give me the impression that you don't like old Marty?"

"Marty? Ahh! Marty! Well, as a matter of fact, Herr Rourke, I do not like him one bit. He is an annoying—"

"Are you searching for the word *prick*, Croenberg?"

"Yes, a prick. Now, if you would step over to the balcony and take in that lovely view for one last time, please."

Michael didn't move. He smoked his cigarette. And he asked Croenberg, "Are you planning to kill me and make it appear that Martin's dead?"

"The thought had crossed my mind, yes. You see, I have always believed that the true test of genius is the ability to take advantage of opportunity, then capitalize on the present rather than vainly plan for a future which may never come."

"Aside from the fact that you're a Nazi and that Nazis are assholes, of course "—Croenberg's eyes hardened and his fist balled slightly more tightly to his gun—"I find you quite engaging. And your philosophy concerning seizing the moment is something with which I wholeheartedly agree. Carpe diem."

"Yes, the dead language, Latin. How appropriate for a man who is soon to be dead to use the dead language. To the balcony, please."

Michael sat where he was. "You don't want me shot. You want me splattered all over the sidewalk. . . ."

"Actually," Croenberg smiled wickedly, "I would more suppose you will be 'splattered,' as you put it, all over the street. Science and mathematics seem to suggest to me that the fall would pull you slightly outward. But, shall we experiment? You will know a split second before I do."

"You can always go first, if you like," Michael offered.

"I find your wit rather engaging as well, and you are correct of course that if I shoot you, my ends will not be so well served as if you merely die from impact. But I will

76

shoot you if I must. Think of it this way, Herr Rourke. If you walk toward the balcony, perhaps you can attempt to disarm me, perhaps even succeed. Otherwise, I must merely pull the trigger."

"Best to squeeze, as I'm sure you know. More accurate shot placement. Don't you think Deitrich Zimmer will be able to tell from the remains that it isn't Martin, but someone else instead?"

"Ohh, he would indeed be able to tell. But, by the time he arrives, which will not be until several hours have passed, I will have succeeded in beginning a process that not even Deitrich Zimmer will be able to stop."

Michael grinned, snapped his fingers, then said, "I know! A coup, right?"

Croenberg smiled with seemingly genuine warmth. "As a matter of fact, yes. You guessed it Herr Rourke. Congratulations."

"I don't understand. You're all Nazis and you all want to start a war to take over the world. And the only way to defeat the Trans-Global Alliance is to go nuclear—"

"I think we have talked sufficiently, Herr Rourke," Croenberg announced, the smile vanishing from his face.

Michael stood up, his cigarette smoked half down. "You think you can do it better, and you don't want to worry about Martin Zimmer when it's all through, right?"

"Something like that." Croenberg gestured with the pistol's muzzle.

Michael started walking. "You still want to hit Pearl Harbor, just like the Japanese did in 1941?"

"Not actually quite like that. They lost their war. We will not. And we wish to avail ourselves of the United States Fleet, not send it to the bottom."

Michael stopped, looking Croenberg straight in the eye. They were dead even now. "Bottom? Whose?"

There was a moment's look of incomprehension in Croenberg's eyes. That was the same moment Michael

77

Rourke chose to snap the cigarette into Croenberg's face and throw himself toward the Nazi, his left hand trying to sweep the gun away from the plane of his body.

That was not entirely successful, Michael Rourke realized in the very next instant.

Chapter Fourteen

The night sky, black as velvet, textured with stars, was magnificently clear.

John Rourke navigated by the stars as he rode north. To maximize on the ability of the horses, he planned to stop for ten minutes every hour, rubbing the animals down and switching mounts. He rode the bay mare now. And she was a good runner.

The countryside rolled gently here and was more normal in appearance, tree cover in broad, deep stands. At the rise where he now paused, he shifted his gaze to the south, seeing the lights behind him again.

They were torches. There seemed to be more than a dozen of them, moving at about his own pace.

He now knew at least part of the story of the men who had fled the gunfight in the bar. The torches could be from no source other than a horse posse, and for no purpose other than to read the ground for the prints of his horses.

These men lived in the Wildlands, of course, and reading sign would be as much a part of life as reading a street sign had been more than six centuries ago. But there was nothing to say that these men were good at reading sign. Someone really good at it wouldn't have needed torches on such a clear night.

The time was not right yet, however.

John Rourke urged his mount ahead, down the slope and into the shallow, dish-shaped valley beyond, ever northward. . . .

Michael Rourke's left side burned, and the smell on the air was from his own flesh.

As he rolled from Croenberg, the Nazi was up instantly to his feet. But Croenberg's right hand was limp and the gun was gone from his grasp.

Michael Rourke, his left side paining him badly enough that there were floaters across his eyes, drew his feet under him and threw himself toward Croenberg's knees. It was hard thinking of anyone as being older, of course, because Michael Rourke had been born in the last quarter of the Twentieth Century, but physically Croenberg was well into his fifties. Despite that, he was tough, agile, and hard. As they struck the floor together, Croenberg's breath went from him in a rush. But so did Michael's as Croenberg's left fist hammered across his jaw.

Michael's head snapped back in the same instant that his right knee smashed upward and caught Croenberg in the groin. The Nazi screamed.

Michael fell back.

As Croenberg, doubled over, sprang toward him, Michael Rourke's right leg snapped forward and upward, the toe of Martin Zimmer's boot catching the Nazi just under the jaw, on the Adam's apple or just above it.

Croenberg's hands went to his throat as he fell back.

Michael Rourke reached for the pistol that had fallen to the floor. He had it, then threw himself onto Croenberg, cracking the pistol down across the gleaming pinkish flesh of the Nazi's skull.

Croenberg's head sagged back, then to the side.

Michael Rourke held the pistol's muzzle to Croenberg's temple, then felt for a pulse. There was one, very strong still from the exertion of the fight. And the air passage seemed clear, Croenberg's breathing shallow but regular.

"Don't want you dead, pal." If all Michael's own efforts and those of The Family should fail, Martin Zimmer's hold on the Eden government would be in jeopardy while Croenberg lived. And one less SS officer would not win or lose a war.

Michael leaned back, organizing his thoughts. There was not very much time. The shot could have been heard, and if Deitrich Zimmer were coming soon, there was much to do.

He thought about his mother, lying near death.

Get Deitrich Zimmer to save her. Then kill the man very dead for what he had done before. . . .

Her Detonics Scoremaster was in her right hand, the hammer cocked, the safety off, and her finger on the trigger. The muzzle was about an inch away from Martin's crotch.

"You would not really shoot your own brother, would you." It wasn't a question, but more of a statement.

Annie Rourke Rubenstein smiled at Martin Zimmer. "I always wanted a baby sister." And she jabbed the muzzle against his testicles.

The smile that had started forming in his eyes vanished. He really believed her.

She could see past him, through the slit where the rain poncho, which was mounded over with snow, and the actual ground met.

There were two vehicles, both of them heavily armored personnel carriers, fully tracked and moving very rapidly.

Hiding beneath the snow was all they could do, and even at that, heat-sensing equipment might find them through body temperature alone.

The women were to her immediate right, in groups of two, probably freezing even more than she was.

Paul and the woman in the stretcher were to her left,

their positions forming a crescent along what was antici-pated to be the least likely path for the vehicles to take.

Both vehicles flew small Nazi flags from their hatch-ways.

"When my people find you, sister dear, I shall person-ally delight in your slow and painful death."

"Gee, Martin, I bet you would've twisted the heads off my Barbie dolls, too, huh? Shut up. And, yes, I know if I fire this pistol, your boys will hear it and we're in deep trouble. Maybe Deitrich Zimmer's such a hotshot surgeon he can put your testicles back together. Go ahead and let's try."

"How our father must admire you, sister dear. You are tough like a man."

"Sex doesn't matter when it comes to believing in what's right, Martin. What's right is right. But the man who raised you preferred to raise you on a pack of lies. You wondered if I'd really pull the trigger. I would. And Daddy is proud of me. And so's my husband."

"The Jew, yes."

She didn't say anything, because if she kept at it and Martin kept at it, too, maybe she really would blow his manhood away.

Chapter Fifteen

In many respects, James Darkwood had always considered himself quite a bit like his illustrious ancestor, Jason Darkwood, the fondness for antiques a common trait. On those occasions when he had to carry a gun (to be found as a civilian in Eden in possession of a firearm was punishable, sometimes by death), he favored a cartridge arm to the more modern hand-held energy devices.

There was a firm in Hawaii that still made such firearms; to this day such guns were quite popular among target shooters and purists, in New Germany according to articles he'd read in magazines devoted to guns and shooting.

He reached under his coat to that cartridge arm now. The gun was very nearly as old a design as one could find that still fired a fixed round. Yet, it was one of the best.

"That man exiting the building. It's either John Rourke or Michael Rourke. And look at the way he's holding his side, Manfred."

"The guard is coming after him," Manfred Kohl responded matter-of-factly.

James Darkwood nodded, saying nothing. He had the gun out. It was a nearly identical duplicate of the classic Colt/Browning model 1911A1, but with similar design modifications to those incorporated into the Detonics .45s carried by John Rourke. Like those guns and the later

Colts—one of Darkwood's hobbies was arms history—this gun was in stainless steel.

And Darkwood doubly trusted the firm that made it— Lancer. Lancer was the company that designed and produced the 9mm Caseless Lancer 2418 A2 pistol, which saw considerable use in the closing years of the War. Jason Darkwood had carried one of those into battle. Manfred Kohl had often commented to him, "Only seven rounds plus one in the chamber; you are insane, James. What if you are in a firefight?"

But those seven rounds were 185-grain jacketed hollow points, the bullet nearly twice the weight of more commonly encountered handgun projectiles in those relatively few handguns that even fired projectiles in this day of energy weapons. The loads were duplicates of those Dr. Rourke had used and still did use in his own guns, as originally made by Federal Cartridge during the Twentieth Century.

At all times, Darkwood carried at least two spare magazines for his Lancer .45 ACP. Should a situation arise beyond twenty-two rounds being sufficient, he was in trouble. But he didn't walk into such a situation by choice. If a firefight should loom, he would take an energy rifle. Going to a gunfight by choice was stupid enough, but going to one by choice armed with only a handgun was insane.

Hawaiian-based Lancer produced various antique firearms from the Nineteenth and Twentieth Centuries, all handcrafted, many of them meticulous duplicates of other guns of Dr. Rourke's together with the appropriate ammunition.

The .45 was in his hand, his thumb poised over the hammer as he started across the street.

Manfred Kohl had his weapon out as well, just under his coat. Darkwood's gun was beside his right thigh as he cocked the hammer and called out to the guard from halfway across the street, "Say, excuse me! Hi! I'm a little lost, I think, and—"

The guard wheeled around toward him, snarling, "Fuck off!"

Whichever Rourke it was walking slightly bent over and in obvious pain—he looked more like Michael Rourke the closer James Darkwood got—turned around and called to the guard, "Return to your post. That is an order."

James Darkwood didn't know what was going on at all, but in his business that was nothing unusual. . . .

Natalia Tiemerovna reined in her mount.

"Stop your horse, Mary Ann," Natalia ordered the girl who rode beside her.

The girl's one admirable quality (under these circumstances, at least) was her quickness to obey, but Natalia felt a growing concern for her as a person. Mary Ann was so used to being abused that she had forgotten, it seemed, how to assert herself as a woman, had she ever known at all.

But now Natalia's attention was drawn to one thing only—the immediate crisis. Two heavily tracked vehicles were just coming over a low rise. If the occupants had not already picked up two mounted riders and the additional horses, visually or with sensing equipment, they would in an instant.

Natalia stood in her stirrups. There was a defile to the north. "Come on! Hurry, Mary Ann!" As she dug in her heels, Natalia wrapped her right hand more tightly in the lead rope for the four mounts she led. "Bring the horses. Don't lose them!" Natalia looked back. Mary Ann was turning her horse toward the defile, the four horses she led were struggling to be free. Natalia made an instant decision.

Natalia drew in the reins of her own animal and, as

Mary Ann struggled past, shifted the lead for the four horses to her left hand, holding that and the reins of her mount as well. Natalia bit off her right outer glove, then reached for the Bali-Song. She wished she had brought along the sword that had been made for her more than a century ago.

The Bali-Song's blade flew open in her fingers, her right arm already arcing downward, severing the lead rope to the four animals Mary Ann had in tow.

"Run for it!" Natalia commanded. Mary Ann's horse vaulted ahead through the snow, toward the defile.

Natalia already had her knife closed, pouching it. She grabbed the glove from her teeth. It was heavy and of a German synthetic that so closely matched real leather it even tasted like it. She slapped the glove across the rump of the nearest of the just-freed horses, the animal bucking once, then running back the way she and Mary Ann had come.

Natalia glanced once toward the armored personnel carriers. A swastika banner was visible on the nearer of the two machines.

Muttering "Damn" under her breath, hauling tight on the lead rope for her own four spare horses, Natalia used the glove like a riding crop across the rump of her own animal, starting it into a loping gallop toward the defile. With any luck, sensors or visual observation from the APCs would pick up the four loose horses and nothing else.

With any luck. . . .

Michael Rourke had Croenberg's little pistol in his right hand. As the guard from the entrance to the high rise started to swing his assault rifle forward toward James Darkwood and Manfred Kohl, Michael put the muzzle of the pistol to the man's head. "Unlike an energy weapon, even a little one like this will punch a hole right through the side of your head."

The guard lowered his weapon. Manfred Kohl, a gun in his right hand, pushed the Eden defense forces trooper into the alley. James Darkwood reached for Michael, saying, "You look like shit."

"Glad somebody noticed." And then Michael Rourke almost started to laugh, but the pain in his side was too intense for that.

Chapter Sixteen

The horsemen who pursued him by torchlight rode relentlessly across the snow. Although John Rourke was easily able to stay ahead of them because he had planned ahead and brought a spare mount, at the pace he had to push both animals, there was no time for resting. At this rate, the horses would be played out in another few hours, as would those ridden by the posse, their mounts probably sooner.

But the fact remained that without a horse, John Rourke knew he would not reach the rendezvous point with the agents from Allied Intelligence. Therefore, aside from his own predicament, Paul and Annie and Natalia would be stranded with Martin Zimmer and the women, one of whom couldn't even walk.

This side of the rift valley, although sparsely populated, seemed to be a dangerous place. The people here whom he had met, constantly on the defensive against the attacks of the Land Pirates, had sunk to the level of their enemies. Mary Ann had clearly been mentally abused before falling victim to the Land Pirates and John Rourke somehow doubted she was atypical. Few of the women he and the others had rescued from the fortress of the Land Pirates seemed to possess anything of culture, or even civility. All seemed worn beyond their years. Transformations such as that did not come about overnight.

John Rourke had rested his mounts as long as he dared now. He climbed aboard the grey. The animals seemed little better cared for than the women around here, and both the grey and the little mare were starting to show signs of fatigue. The cold, intense with the night, didn't help matters.

John Rourke urged his animals ahead. In his mind, he was constructing a contingency plan to alleviate the deteriorating situation. . . .

The "safe house" was, indeed, a house; how safe it was remained to be seen. It was one of the homes built better than fifty years ago when Eden had gone through a single-family housing boom. Deep within Eden City itself, it was now substandard and most of the houses in the area were abandoned. There was no electricity. Synth-fuel lamps burned at either end of the table.

There was no glass in the windows anywhere, the openings boarded over. But blankets, by contrast new looking, were hung inside to prevent any light from showing.

Six centuries ago, the area would have been called a slum. Michael Rourke had read about such places. Now he was experiencing it. . . .

"Pearl Harbor?" James Darkwood repeated, but as a question.

Michael Rourke nodded his head. Kohl was trained as a medic and set about cleaning the wound on Michael's side. "This is not too bad, Michael. A little rest and taking it easy for a while, you should be fine."

"You've gotta get people alerted to what's happening, but first you have to send out some sort of a rescue party," Michael told them. He'd refused any sort of pain killer while Kohl worked on his wound. To risk dulling his senses now could spell disaster in more ways than he could calculate.

"Are you sure they weren't aware of who you were, Michael? And this Martin guy is really your brother?"

Michael looked squarely at Darkwood. "Martin Zimmer is some sort of product of Deitrich Zimmer. He has to be. Whether it's the way Martin was raised or there was genetic tampering or . . . I don't know. But the point is, Croenberg wouldn't have come to kill me himself if anybody else had known. He was banking on the idea that I'd at least temporarily be mistaken for Martin Zimmer, long enough for him and his people—"

"You mean Croenberg and his 'cronies,' " James Darkwood suggested with a smile.

"You laugh, fine. But Croenberg wants the power for himself and his faction But none of that is important now. The deal about an attack on Pearl Harbor was real. Croenberg can't substantially change the plans without a reason. What's he gonna say?"

James Darkwood nodded his head. "He can't very well say that he knew you weren't Martin and tried to kill you so he could organize a coup. And, if he figures something may have happened to Martin, Croenberg's better off not saying anything about what happened, or anything more than he has to in order to cover for the fight you two had. You're right. If the Pearl Harbor thing is really on, there may be some minor detail changes. He could get away with that. He might even move up the timetable. But he can't cancel it out."

Michael Rourke controlled his breathing in order to control the pain in his side. "Get some people out after my dad and Natalia and everybody. We get Dad, he'll know what to do."

"Getting a rescue party up is not that easy," Kohl said as he affixed an adhesive dressing over the wound. "Getting over the rift valley is dangerous. Unless we fly so

90

high that we'll be picked up on Eden defense sensors and get shot down anyway, we have to keep very low. That means that a storm over the valley can destroy us."

Michael Rourke was trying to think. There had to be a way.

James Darkwood lit a cigarette. As he exhaled, he said, "I think I know how we can handle this. If HQ approves it, it'll work and expedite the whole thing."

Michael blamed it on the pain, but he didn't understand. "What's your headquarters have to approve?"

"An incursion on Eden soil. Technically, at least, the entire continental United States with the exception of Alaska is an Eden protectorate, even though west of the rift valley isn't part of Eden itself. We've got submarines off the west coast. One of the patrol sectors covers from what used to be Chihuahua up along Arizona to as far north as Reno Harbor. If I can get a commando team flown in, they can locate your family, evacuate them and the women, then fly your father and the rest of them right out to Pearl."

"Then do it," Michael told him. "Some of those women will need medical attention. And you're going to have to find a safe place to stash Martin Zimmer. We need him for our own reasons."

"You stay with Michael," Kohl offered. "I will get out of the city and make the satellite uplink."

James Darkwood's eyes showed worry. Michael forced himself to stand up. "We'll all go, then get out of Eden City and find some transportation to Pearl Harbor."

"You should not be moving about," Manfred Kohl advised soberly.

"I should not be living in this century, either, should I?" Michael felt mildly nauseous, but he wasn't about to mention it.

* * *

Natalia lay in the snow, the stock of her short-barreled assault rifle extended and snug against her shoulder. The weapon would be useless against the armored personnel carriers, of course, but not against the occupants, should they emerge.

The two tracked vehicles had stopped some time ago, near the hoofprints. Lights played over the snow, but that was all.

Mary Ann lay beside her. "If we give up," the girl said in a low, hoarse whisper, "they won't murder us. They'll wanna fuck us and then we'll be all right."

Natalia looked at her, stunned.

"When the Land Pirates hit us, they killed a whole lot. Me, I figures what'll work and it does," Mary Ann went on. "When they breaks in where I hid, I ripped open my dress and let 'em see my tits. Then I says, 'Who wants a blow?' And—"

Despite the possibility that the sound would be heard, Natalia slapped the girl hard across the face.

"What the—?"

"Listen to me, Mary Ann," Natalia said through her clenched teeth. "Sex is something two people have because both people want it, not something a woman does to make an excuse for her to be kept alive. We're not surrendering to the men in those armored personnel carriers. And they won't take us without a fight. And, if they take us, the only way they'll 'take us' in the way you are talking about is to kill us or drug us so we're unconscious. Some men enjoy sex that way—it's called necrophilia—but most men don't. If you try anything else, I will kill you. Because you would be better off dead with self-respect than being alive without it. Is that clear?"

Tears streamed down Mary Ann's cheeks, one redder than the other where Natalia had slapped it. But Mary Ann nodded. . . .

* * *

Paul Rubenstein moved through the snow on knees and elbows, the Schmiesser in both hands just forward of his jaw. He was near the height of the rise and did not want to risk silhouetting himself there and attracting attention. But he had to make certain that the armored personnel carriers had moved on far enough ahead to get the women out of hiding in the snow before they froze to death.

But, in the next instant, his ears confirmed what his eyes could not yet see.

The APCs were near.

Finally attaining the height of the rise, he kept his head very low, furrowing out a narrow channel in a ridge of hard-packed snow so he could see.

The machines had stopped. Powerful lights played over the ground, where there were markings along the way.

Paul pushed his submachine gun onto his back, then uncased the German binoculars. They had vision intensification capabilities and he used that now, careful to avoid looking directly into one of the lights and temporarily blinding himself.

Instead, he focused on the markings in the snow.

As a kid growing up on Air Force bases, it wasn't the sort of thing he'd exactly seen every day. But since The Night Of The War he'd learned a lot of things. And this was one of the simplest.

The markings in the snow were horses' hoofprints.

There was nothing to suggest that bands of wild horses lived in this barren snow country. That meant that John and Natalia and that crazy girl, Mary Ann, had made them. And either John or Natalia was out there somewhere on the way back with help.

Paul Rubenstein put down his glasses and waited. There was nothing else he could do.

Chapter Seventeen

He had given away most of his warm clothing to the women and wore only a heavy woolen sweater over his thermal shirt. John Thomas Rourke, his body shaking with the cold, lay in the snow.

He suffered from a lack of appropriate equipment. The German assault rifle, firing a caseless cartridge and due for phaseout over the latest energy rifle, was decent but not the sort of thing he liked for a sniping situation. The cartridge was less a potential manstopper than the 5.56mm round used in his CAR-15 and similar AR-15/ M-16 weapons systems. And, it went against his grain for him to enter into a sniping situation with the necessity to burst fire.

Yet, he could not trust one solitary round to do the job of nailing a man wearing heavy winter gear.

The rifle did not meet the terrain and situation requirements.

His alternatives to the rifle were less than satisfactory. There were nine men in the party. Although the quality of the arms they carried could not be vouched for, the abundance of them was obvious through his binoculars.

Indeed, so much less than satisfactory were his alternatives that they ceased to exist.

John Rourke brought the rifle to his shoulder. It didn't have the feel of the Steyr-Mannlicher SSG, nor even that of his CAR-15 or an ordinary M-16. The stock, a bullpup type, was ideal for close range maneuverability, but less than ideal for precision riflery.

And John Rourke suddenly wondered if he were becoming an anachronism.

He lived in a world so far removed from his own time that the only things about it which seemed at all familiar were brutality, greed, and the occasional incident of human nobility.

If he could save Sarah, somehow. . . . He had never realized how much he loved her until she was gone. His desire for Natalia—it was love, genuine enough—was not what he felt for his wife. He desired Sarah. He loved Sarah. And, unlike Natalia, Sarah was a part of him and he was a part of her, too. If—he wanted to believe in *when*—but if he could bring her back, he would go with her someplace and start all over again, leaving this behind them.

He had fought for longer than any man had ever fought.

And he was tired of fighting.

Peace on Earth would only be achieved when man was absent from Earth. Perhaps he was becoming a cynic, but at least he was being honest with himself. As long as one man had something another did not, there would be strife. To make all men totally, absolutely equal—the dream of Marxists and Utopians and others since the beginning of the modern era and likely well earlier than that—was impossible except when gauged by the lowest common denominator. All men could be poor, all men could be without property or substance, all men could be denied the most basic of human freedoms, all men could be slaves.

And that was the only way.

Equality under the law and equality in fact were two entirely different matters.

All men were, in fact, created equal.

95

They became what they became, some good and some bad. But most were somewhere between the two opposite poles of morality, most little concerned with anything outside their own immediate sphere.

People were and always would be, as long as they were people, ready to kill.

The immediate now was as fine an example of that truth as he could have conceived of. His life was more valuable to him than the lives of the nine men who pursued him. His life was valuable to him not only because of his desire to continue living, but also because hinged upon his survival were the lives of several people he loved.

Toward the end of living for himself and for those he loved, he had now to take something that only God could return in the hereafter. He'd taken many lives and, as long as he lived, would likely be forced to continue the practice.

What was wrong with the world was definitely the infestation that lived upon it.

"Bitter, John Rourke?" John Rourke queried of himself and the night.

There was no response. He already knew the answer and the night ignored him.

Through the little integral scope in the rifle's carrying handle, he watched the first man he would shoot.

He could not see the face clearly. That was good.

Chapter Eighteen

Port Reno, Nevada, to Emma Shaw's way of thinking, was the drain trap beneath Earth's toilet. At least the same sort of thing accumulated there.

A cold wind blew out of the mountains and she snapped up the collar of her bomber jacket. Marie Hayes and Ward Aldridge flanked her. As they turned the corner, a little boy ran up to them. "Hey, want some sex?" He took a step back from them and the sandwich screen image on his chest was more easily visible. "Whatchya like?" And then he looked at Marie.

He touched one of the buttons on the console carried on a plastic belt at his waist, just beneath the screen, and the image flickered. There were two women, one Chinese and the other white. They were naked except for studded black leather dog collars and they were going at each other as if there were no tomorrow.

Ward Aldridge asked, "Can women really do that to one another?"

The boy pushed another button. At least his sandwich screens had something for every taste. The subject this time was a black woman, evidently to appeal to Ward, and she was having sex with a machine. There were machine sex shops all over Port Reno, of course, and all over the "civilized" world as well. The machines themselves were bisexual, one end fitted with a realistic-looking dildo and the other with a realistic-looking vaginal-like opening. They were pneumatic and could keep going longer than their customers could, as long as enough coins of whatever realm were deposited to keep the power turned on.

"Get lost, little guy," Emma told the kid. The boy shrugged his skinny shoulders and walked off. The backside of the sandwich screen showed a different program, quick cuts of something that looked like a Roman orgy with titles superimposed for the name of the "Ranch," these in English, Russian, Chinese, and German, the four principal languages.

There was even a road map showing how to get to the establishment.

Emma dug her hands into her jacket pockets and walked on.

Along the strip, the boy with his sandwich screens blended in with at least a half dozen other kids of similar size and age and in the same racket. People were everywhere, a good percentage of them prostitutes of every description, including women in male drag and men in female drag.

The casinos were lit up so brightly that it was almost possible to forget it was night.

" 'All Nude Review.' There you go, I'm gone," Ward Aldridge laughed. Then he really did stop walking, just staring up at the video marquee.

Emma Shaw had to admit the girls looked beautiful. She looked at Ward Aldridge and asked him, "So, why are you waiting?"

"Hey, I just don't know if I should leave—"

"Two unescorted ladies to fend for themselves?" Marie queried.

Ward shrugged his big shoulders and grinned good-naturedly.

"Two unescorted United States Armed forces officers?" Marie pressed. "I'm a Marine like you, remember? I can look after Emma, seeing she's only Navy. So, what's your problem?"

Emma was more compassionate to Ward Aldridge's moral dilemma and his male ego. She said, "Look, Ward, we've all got beepers and even if we wanted to, regs say we can't hit this port unless we're armed. So, we're fine. But, if you get in trouble, just hit your beeper and we'll bail you out, okay?" Emma added, laughing.

His black skin looked almost purple under the neon lights as he said, "I mean it. You guys be careful, okay?"

Emma took a step back and placed her right hand over her heart. "Honest injun, Ward. Marie and I were on our way to the public library, anyway."

"No public library here, girl," Ward laughed, then shot them a wave as he started in under the marquee.

Then he was gone, lost in the crowd. Emma took her hands out of her pockets and rubbed them together. "So, Marie! Which way to the library?"

"Yeah, right," Marie answered, starting to laugh. "How about some food? Then we can figure out what we wanna do."

"So long as it's not Chinese. Around here, God knows what you'd be eating in the chop suey."

"Amen," Marie laughed.

Emma spotted a flashing neon sign, smaller than most of the others. But its message struck a peculiarly respondent note in her heart. "Pizza!"

Together, they ran across the strip, dodging the electric cars and the horse carriages.

John Rourke gradually increased the pressure against the bullpup-actioned assault rifle's unsatisfactory single trigger.

The rifle moved almost not at all as the cartridge fired.

As he had suspected, the sights were a little off. The bullet he'd aimed for the first man's neck struck through the jaw. "Shit," Rourke murmured, summing up his sentiments as he swung the muzzle of the rifle, settled the scope—he didn't quite like its universal eye relief—and fired again. He held a little low on this shot, aiming for a midpoint between the sternum and the Adam's apple of his second man. The bullet tore through the Adam's apple.

The first man's horse, the man still alive and clinging to it, raced past Rourke's field of view. Rourke took a quick shot, hitting the man somewhere in center of mass, pitching him out of the saddle.

He fired his fourth round on the third man, again one of the ones farther from his position. The shot buckled the man over but didn't knock him out of the saddle. It took a fifth shot to do that.

John Rourke had always detested sloppiness but prided himself on meeting the parameters of whatever situation arose. He flicked the rifle's selector to full auto.

Gunfire, ill aimed, came toward Rourke's position as he fired on the fourth man, punching him out of the saddle with a five round burst.

The fifth man was aiming some sort of rifle—or trying to at least—the animal under him jostling side to side, making accurate fire impossible.

John Rourke was solidly embedded in snow-covered rocks. When he fired, the rifle flew from the fifth man's hands and the man's body tumbled back out of the saddle and across his horse's flanks, the animal rearing with the sudden shifting of weight and pressure.

Two of the men were out of the saddle, firing long guns. A couple of bullets zinged across the rocks about three feet from Rourke's position.

Rourke returned fire, two bursts to each man, putting the men down dead or close to death. He rolled onto his back, tearing the partially spent magazine from the assault rifle's action, sliding a fresh forty-rounder

100

up the well. There was already a round chambered.

Rourke swung back into position as the last two men, both on foot, fell to cover.

The burst of gunfire that tore into the rocks and snow a few inches from Rourke's face was either the act of a decent marksman or dumb luck. Rourke wouldn't gamble on the latter. He laid down suppressive fire, keeping the two men at bay. One of them ran from cover. Rourke fired and missed. The man grabbed for his animal, put a pistol to its head, and fired, crashing the beast down, then dropping behind it for cover.

The two survivors had a modest cross-fire position now, and if they eventually got the range right, Rourke might find himself in trouble.

Rourke sprayed out the rest of the assault rifle's magazine, the dead horse's body bouncing with the multiple impacts, some of the bullets getting through fat and tissue, however. The man behind the horse seemed to stand upright for a split second, then fell back, his rifle discharging in a long burst into the already-mutilated animal.

One man remained.

John Rourke loaded a fresh magazine up the well, then brought his weapon back on line.

Torches the men had carried smoked and sizzled in the snow. Several of the horses had run off, but three of them remained, meandering about the fire zone as if nothing were happening.

The last man was up, darting out from the rocks behind which he'd hidden to one of the horses, firing a half-dozen shots from a rifle. None of the rounds struck anywhere near Rourke.

There was a decision to make. If Rourke shot the horse, he could easily shoot the man. But the horse had nothing to do with the problems between John Rourke and this man he had never met.

Life was precious.

John Rourke waited, keeping the scope settled on where he hoped the man would be. The horse was still between Rourke and his target.

This was taking too long.

Rourke made a decision, swung the muzzle of his rifle, and fired, bullets tearing into the snow and rocks inches away from the animal's hind legs.

The horse bolted forward.

The man fell, sprawling into the snow.

John Rourke fired, killing the man.

Rourke waited.

There was no need to consult the Rolex on his wrist. He simply counted off seconds, surveying the bodies through his rifle's scope, watching for the slightest sign of movement.

After three minutes had passed, John Rourke edged back from his perch and stood.

He would go down into the little dugout valley and check the men. Any who lived, he would provide whatever emergency treatment circumstances allowed. If none lived, things would go more easily and more quickly.

He was shivering badly from the cold. Hopefully, he would find a marginally clean coat or jacket that would provide him some warmth.

He started down from the rocks, leaving his mounts where they were.

Chapter Nineteen

The one good result Emma Shaw could point to from the five centuries of warfare that had nearly destroyed the planet was the fact that a peculiar little fish known as the anchovy was apparently extinct. The thought of putting a fish on a pizza was disgusting in the extreme. Shrimp were okay, but not a fish. But she had read about the practice and seen old video movies in which the fish were actually put on pizzas. According to a boy she'd gone out with while at the Naval Academy, the anchovy was salty-tasting. He had been studying ichthyology, so she guessed that somehow his dissertation on the anchovy was valid.

This pizza, reasonably good, was also reasonably plain. She'd learned that in ports around the Pacific—one should never eat something unless it was unmistakably identifiable. Hence, this pizza had roast beef and onion over the cheese, along with green peppers. Sausage or ground meat was to be looked at with a jaundiced eye.

She drank cola because, although she had shore leave, her unit was on alert.

Marie, like Ward Aldridge a Marine captain, was saying between mouthfuls of pizza, "I don't see any choice. This asshole Martin's a clearcut aggressor, got a war machine like this planet hasn't seen in over a hundred years and he's basically telling every world leader to go screw. We gotta take him out before he tries taking us out."

"There've been lots of tin plate dictators," Emma said, freeing another piece of pizza from the pan. "After a while, they get to be a real problem, but by the time governments figure it out, it's usually too late and the mistake costs a lot of lives."

"Martin lives in Eden City, right? So why not put a lot of people into Eden City real fast and hit him? You Navy guys fly us in, hang around for a few hours, maybe take a little target practice on their anti-aircraft installations, stuff like that, then fly us out again. Piece of cake."

"Do they teach you guys that . . . in the Marines, I mean? To have egos like that?" Emma laughed.

Maria started to laugh and almost choked. "You saying we couldn't do it?"

"Ohh, we could do it, but it's not going to be that easy, Marie. He's got manpower, technology, and no supply problems. Remember, we have to bring the war to him. The terrain is in his favor, too. So many mountains around there, short of nuclear weapons, how do you get at somebody so well entrenched."

"Well, you Navy guys bob in there and dump a lot of conventional explosives."

Emma stared at her piece of pizza. "And what do we respond with when he uses his nuclear weapons and his gas? The same? Why does history have to repeat itself?" She realized she was still staring at a piece of pizza, which was quite unlikely to provide her with an intelligent answer to her question.

104

Marie started to say something.

But their beepers went off simultaneously.

A trilling sound, like a bird whistling, would mean they were being called back to duty. This sound, a buzz, meant that someone else who was set for the same frequency was trying to make contact.

Marie had her beeper out first, switching off the sound and punching up the antenna. "This is Captain Hayes. Come in."

The words that came back were hard to hear with the beeper beside Marie's right ear, but Emma Shaw recognized the voice. It was Ward Aldridge. . . .

Two of the blankets, Eden military surplus, seemed marginally clean. The coats of the dead men were either threadbare or full of holes, in most cases both. John Rourke took the two blankets and cut holes through their centers, then pulled them on like ponchos, one over the other. He cinched them around his waist with his gunbelt, to hold in some warmth.

Of the weapons the dead men had carried, none were of decent quality except for one rifle. The weapon was old, from the last war, and less than a half-dozen rounds of ammunition for its solitary magazine were on the owner's body.

Rourke left the weapons, freed the horses, and led his own mounts up along the ridge to a point where it flattened out a little and there was less danger of a slip. He swung up into the saddle on the little mare.

Both animals were rested now, and while he'd tethered them during his attack on his pursuers, he'd put on their feed bags as well.

Nothing would compensate for the cold and the duration of the ride, but under the circumstances, the animals were fit enough. John Rourke started north again.

Chapter Twenty

Emma Shaw kept her slice of pizza in her left hand so she could get to her gun with her right as she walked beside Marie Hayes, trying not to look hurried, back across the street that divided the strip, toward the place with the all-nude review where Ward Aldridge had gone and was now looking at potentially serious trouble.

The Intell people, rumor had it, believed that Eden had groups of terrorists working as part of a worldwide network, their mission to disrupt and destabilize through as violent a means as possible. There were prominent people being assassinated all over the Allied world. There were robberies, bombings, and the occasional kidnapping for ransom.

A group of guys who had Eden Defense Forces written all over them had drifted into the strip joint over the last forty-five minutes and, according to Ward Aldridge, looked to be heavily armed.

Everyone in the Wildlands who could afford to buy a weapon traveled armed, and those who could not afford to made one. Those who went weaponless often paid a high price.

Emma Shaw and Marie Hayes reached the other side of the street, Emma's eyes moving along the curb, looking for signs that something was about to go down.

Aside from a couple of military surplus internal combustion vehicles parked on the opposite side of the street from the strip joint, there was nothing out of the ordinary. Internal combustion vehicles were common enough in the Wildlands, where population density was light and electric recharge stations might be few and far between.

Even with a poor miles-per-gallon ratio, something in the fifties or so, enough synth-fuel could be carried to cross the width of the continent from one of the farthest points west, like Port Reno, to New Charleston on the east coast.

Emma finished her pizza and tossed the last bite of crust into a trash can.

In another time and another place, the logical thing for Ward Aldridge to have done would have been to call the local police with his suspicions. But many places in the Wildlands had no law enforcement at all because there was no law. Port Reno had cops, but they were worse than any criminal could be, a mixture of ex-Eden Defense Forces personnel and other men, probably some of them onetime Land Pirates. They enforced the edicts of the casino and skin parlor owners, not any sort of law.

Like a small, private mercenary army, they worked solely on behalf of their employers. And, the trouble was, again according to Allied Intelligence, the Port Reno Constabulary might well be in league with the Eden-backed terrorists. As a free port of call and with the largest airport facilities west of the rift valley, Port Reno was a transfer point for almost everyone traveling from one point on the globe to another.

Two burly men, obviously armed with large energy pistols slung to their bodies, stepped into the doorway as Emma and Marie started inside. "If you's comin' to hook, gotta see—"

Emma looked at the one who'd spoken, a six foot or so Chinese with a shaved head and rippling muscles under his Hawaiian-style shirt. "Look at me, big man," Emma Shaw told him. "What's this uniform insignia read? Commander, United States Navy. See that?"

The Chinese stepped away, and Emma and Marie passed by him and the second door guard, into the strip joint.

Ordinary logic would have dictated that when Ward Aldridge realized there was the potential for trouble, he'd have walked out. Emma had always respected Ward's judgment ever since she'd first met him as an upper classman at the Academy, and his judgment was not in question here.

As they passed through the doorway and into the club, she saw the reason Ward had called them on their beepers rather than walked out. There were at least three dozen servicemen in the bar, enlisted men who were, by Port Reno regulation, unarmed. Since Eden Forces and Allied Forces used the port, the Port Reno businessmen had decreed that no uniformed personnel could be armed while in the city. United States regulations dictated that all commissioned officers be armed at all times, so the enlisted men and women traveled weaponless and the officers broke the Port Reno regulations by order, trying to watch out for the enlisted personnel.

A good seventy-five percent of the people on the club's floor were male. Nude dancers performed on a carousel stage that slowly revolved into and out of view, some obvious hookers and the nearly nude waitresses representing the female side. Emma felt out of place, not to mention looking it, her outfit consisting of medium-heel low-quarters, nylons, khaki A-line skirt, khaki uniform shirt, her A-2 jacket, and her hat. The hat, a classic cloth envelope that dated back to World War I and

109

looked stupid on nearly everyone who wore it, especially a woman, was tucked into her uniform belt.

Marie, who had a peculiar fondness for hats, wore hers with her hair piled on top of her head beneath it, just like a girl out of a World War II movie.

Except for the nude dancers, some of whom wore feathers, and the waitresses, who wore skimpy transparent halter tops and bikini bottoms, the rest of the women were dressed in the current fashion. In the magazines, it was called "Neo-Sixties." The look took three routes. There was the basic look, that just meant that skirts were way shorter and sometimes a funny hat was added, or instead of a dress at all a skintight jumpsuit was worn (Emma liked those). Then there was the sweetheart look, which meant that even with the short skirts the attire was overall very lacy and frilly. Lastly, there was the really avant-garde. This latter style made all the women who wore it look like hookers, at least to Emma Shaw's way of thinking. Their outfits consisted of micro-mini skirts, usually of a fabric made to resemble leather, textured stockings, and thigh-top high-heeled boots. All this with a skimpy top and lots of junk jewelry made the amateurs awfully hard to distinguish from the professionals. Most of the other women she saw here were into micro-minis and boots, and if her first assumption that they were hookers was incorrect, they certainly dressed the part.

Emma followed Marie toward one of the two long bars. The bars were set at an acute angle, forming an apex-less triangle, the entrance itself where the apex would have been. The revolving stage formed the base. The dance floor, together with ridiculously small round tables, filled the area within the triangle, with loud disco music blaring from speakers the size of small aircraft.

The idea behind the positioning of the bars was obvious. Anyone who sat at either one could see the show on the revolving stage, either by swiveling around on his stool or by looking over the bar into the system of mirrors behind and above the respective bar.

Ward Aldridge occupied a stool by the entrance on the right-hand side. He must have been watching the two women approaching in the mirrors. As they joined him, without turning around, he asked, "Buy you ladies a cola?"

"Sure . . . hey, our kidneys are up for it," Emma said, sitting down beside him on the right, Marie taking the stool on his left.

Ward Aldridge didn't have to point out the men he thought appeared suspicious. Emma Shaw was already spotting them herself. It amused her to consider that she was probably the only serviceperson in the place, aside from Marie, who wasn't staring raptly at the stage. As she worked her eyes over the bars and the table area, searching for the questionable patrons of the type Ward Aldridge was worried over, she saw servicemen, mostly marines and some sailors, all of them unarmed if they abided by regs. Not to do so could mean disciplinary action.

If an Eden terror squad were planning a hit on the place, it wouldn't be the first time that American servicemen were their victims. There had been an incident in Rio de Janeiro on the South American Atlantic coast three weeks ago in which fifteen Allied service personnel—Americans from Mid-Wake and Hawaii and Germans—were killed and forty-three others wounded. Although Eden disavowed the action, even condemning it at the Geneva talks that seemed to always be going on, Eden terrorists had to have been responsible.

She was a fan of the great detective novels of the Twentieth Century, and the terrorist act in Rio fit the

111

Eden M.O. perfectly.

She looked at Ward as her cola arrived, took a sip of it, then tossed her hair back from her shoulders as she asked, "So, what'll we do, big guy?"

"If we start something and I'm wrong, we've created a diplomatic incident with Eden. If I knew what to do, I'd be doing it, Emma."

Emma Shaw nodded, thinking.

Marie suggested, "How about the Shore Patrol?"

"Same thing," Ward told her. "Our boys go into action, diplomatic incident time. But we can't just sit here."

"Wait a minute," Emma said. There was a permanent Shore Patrol Station at the harbor. All the spots along the strip had the number and could reach the station instantly in the event Allied service personnel started trouble. It was just standard procedure. "If the Shore Patrol is called in by us, it's a diplomatic incident maybe. If the club management calls in the Shore Patrol, it's another story."

Ward just looked at her, then started to smile.

Emma bowed her head and batted her eyelashes, saying, "Thank you very much." Then she slipped off her bar stool and started walking along the length of the bar, toward the end nearest the stage. There were a half-dozen Russian merchant seamen at that end, and although Russia was a member of the Trans-Global Alliance and a good friend of the United States on an official level, there was no love lost between U.S. and Russian personnel at the personal level.

She stopped in front of the largest of the six Russian seamen, turned, and slapped him in the face. "You son of a bitch! You can't talk to a woman like that!"

The man looked at her dumbfounded. His English, heavily accented, was pretty good. "What is wrong with

112

you, Commander?"

"Filth!" She slapped him again, harder, feeling sorry for the guy as she did it.

From the edges of her peripheral vision, she could see some of the U.S. service personnel starting to turn around and stare, some of them even standing.

She shouted at the Russian sailor again, "Look, Ivan, maybe you can talk that way to your own women, but you can't talk that way to an American girl! Put 'em up!" And she took a swing, not a slap this time, but her right fist balled up. He dodged her and she lost her balance a little, almost falling on her pride.

But the Russian seaman did what she'd been hoping he'd do since she slapped him the first time. He shoved her.

Despite his size, he didn't shove her hard enough to knock her down, but she took the shove as if he had and sent herself sprawling onto the floor.

Then she screamed, "You beast!"

There was a blur of khaki as a U.S. Marine lance corporal stepped up, offered her his hand, and said, "Ma'am." She let him help her up, making herself cry (she'd learned the trick in high school when she went out for drama club). "Don't worry, Commander," the lance corporal said. Then he turned around to the big Russian and socked him right across the jaw, slamming the Russian into his friend beside him.

The friend took a swing at the lance corporal, but somebody—a U.S. sailor this time—caught the Russian's arm in mid arc and spun him around, then fired two right jabs and a left hook, putting the Russian's lights out.

And in the next instant, almost everybody was fighting—the Russians at the bar, the American service personnel, the Port Reno civilians, even some of the hookers. All around Emma, chairs and synth-glass bottles flew through the air.

She dodged one, ducked another, then hitched up her skirt and kneed one of the Port Reno civilians in the crotch as he grabbed for her. Ward Aldridge caught him, reverse jackknifed him to a standing position, and crossed his jaw with a short left.

Ward shouted, "Shore Patrol's coming! Shore Patrol!"

And Emma Shaw knew his reasoning. This way, the GI's would get out and not have to spend the evening in the brig.

She looked around and saw Marie crack a synth-glass bottle over a civilian's head.

But past Marie, near the entrance, she saw several of the military-looking civilians Ward had pegged as Eden terrorists making for the door. She tapped Ward on the shoulder and he turned around so fast she thought he was going to take a poke at her. "What?"

"Those guys you thought were terrorists. Let's follow them."

"With what?"

"Desert cab?"

"And I betchya I know who picks up the tab. Right?"

"Well, it's the gentlemanly thing to do," she told him, batting her eyelashes again.

"Shit. Let's go!" Ward ran for the door, presumably to hail a desert cab.

Emma Shaw looked for Marie. But her friend wasn't there. "Marie! Marie?!"

The fighting was slowing down, most of the GI's running out onto the strip. But there was no sign of Marie.

Although she'd probably hit the bricks like everybody else, Emma was getting a funny feeling in the pit of her stomach and it wasn't from the pizza. She ran toward the door, shouting, "Out of the way! Out of the way!"

114

Those servicemen who looked her way at all deferred to her commander's rank and her sex, but most didn't even bother to look.

Pushing and shoving, she made her way into the bright lights of the strip and saw Ward Aldridge instantly, almost wrestling one of the half-track desert cabs to a halt in the middle of the street.

And then she looked to the other side of the strip, to the two Eden military surplus half-tracks. She saw a flash of khaki being dragged through the fuselage opening just as the drop down hatch started to raise. "Holy shit!"

Emma Shaw grabbed her hair with her left hand, pulling it back and away from her face. She ran her tongue across her lower lip, then shouted, "Ward! Ward! They got Marie!"

Ward wheeled about toward the two military surplus vehicles and just stood there, like herself, she guessed, not knowing what to do.

But then she knew what to do.

Still holding her hair with her left hand, she drew her pistol from the shoulder holster under her armpit with her right hand, then fired it three times into the night sky. "Yo! Navy! Marines!" She realized she was standing on her toes. "The guys in those half-tracks got Captain Marie Hayes in there with them. Get every vehicle you can and block the road! Move it!"

The second half-track was still loading, four men running across the strip toward it, brandishing weapons but not firing. Emma Shaw, her pistol in her hand, started to run toward the four Eden terrorists.

At the far left edge of her peripheral vision, she saw the desert cab Ward Aldridge had flagged down starting to move. She shot a full glance to her left. The cab driver, a woman about Emma's own age, was standing there in the middle of the street, shaking her fist. The cab was aimed right for the still-lowered door of the second half-track, Ward Aldridge at the wheel.

Desert cabs were used all along the west coast. They were converted half-tracks, much like the vehicles the Eden terrorists drove, only stripped of the heavier armor and fitted with more comfortable seats, the engines worked over for better top speed.

The desert cab Ward drove was coming on fast. Two of the four men racing toward their still unbuttoned half-track spun toward the desert cab and opened fire with energy rifles. But energy rifles were strictly anti-personnel weapons and next to useless against light armor unless the hits were repeated and concentrated in one spot heavy enough to melt the armor.

Ward was zigzagging the desert cab as he drove it toward the men, making it impossible for their fire to penetrate his armor. Emma stopped running and brought her pistol up into a point shoulder position. Officers could select their own personal sidearm and she had selected the Lancer 2570 A2-C, the "C," or Compact, and its full-size counterpart the only projectile-firing handguns still in the inventory. It was the choice of the Marine Raiders and the SEALs, and was favored by the Honolulu Police Department as well.

Her father was a Honolulu cop and so was her older brother. She'd cut her teeth on the 2570 A2-C and had stuck with it.

Now she squeezed the trigger and dropped the nearer of the four Eden terrorists shooting at Ward in the desert cab. Ward ran over a second man and, involuntarily, Emma Shaw turned her head for an instant, recoiling from the sight. She'd never shot anybody before in her life, but at the moment putting out the lights out on a terrorist hadn't sunk in enough to bother her.

116

But seeing a man turned into a smudge of grease about the same thickness of the pizza she'd just split with Marie Hayes was another thing.

As she looked back, the two remaining men were running toward the second vehicle, which was already in motion, its side loading door still open, dragging along the street surface and making a shower of sparks.

It was picking up speed.

The desert cab Ward Aldridge drove was nearly at top speed.

As the two vehicles met, Ward's desert cab drove onto and stopped dead on the ramplike door. The half-track spun around about ninety degrees and stayed there, Ward's desert cab sitting on its door.

The street that bisected the entertainment strip was filling up with vehicles from both directions, more desert cabs, electric cars, and everything else the GI's had been able to put into motion to block the escape of the two half-tracks. But from the direction of the docks, there were Shore Patrol vehicles coming.

Emma started running again, dropping into a crouch beside the man she'd shot, feeling the knee go out in her right stocking as she did. She grabbed up the dead man's energy rifle—she really had killed him. A shiver went up her spine and there was a slightly sick feeling in her stomach. The energy rifle in her right hand, the 9mm Lancer Caseless pistol in her left, she charged toward the first military surplus half-track.

It was stopped, too, and the door was opening.

She saw some of the men from the bar, and between them she saw Marie Hayes. Marie's hat was gone and her hair had fallen down. Her jacket was off her shoulders and over her arms, exposing the harness from her shoulder holster.

One of the terrorists shouted, "Back off or we kill the

Marine bitch!"

The Shore Patrol vehicles were stopping, uniformed SPs piling out, bristling with weaponry.

An electric staff car pulled up behind the wedge the SP vehicles had made. Emma Shaw recognized the man who got out of it. He was Captain Edmund Rahn, not only the youngest captain in the fleet and the sexiest hunk in the Navy, but the most obnoxiously arrogant and conceited man she'd ever met. He was also her commanding officer.

He took off his cap as he passed through the ranks of SPs, running his fingers through his dark, wavy hair. "Shaw! What the hell is going on here?"

She couldn't very well come to attention or even salute, because she was holding a gun in each hand and they were both leveled at the terrorists. "Sir, we've got a situation here. These men are Eden terrorists. Captain Aldridge, Captain Hayes, and myself discovered them preparing to attack one of the clubs here on the strip. We started a fight in order to evacuate the building and preempt any enemy action. They took Captain Hayes hostage, sir."

"Tell me this is some sort of stunt for a movie, Shaw. And Captain Aldridge is just playing a part. So that desert cab that's having sex with that half-track is just a prop."

"No, sir! They really are having—I mean, Captain Aldridge used the desert cab to stop the vehicles, sir. The personnel who assisted us in evacuating the club were—"

"Why the hell I gave any of you clowns liberty at Port Reno is beyond me. . . ."

Emma Shaw couldn't help it. "You were ordered to, sir, by Admiral of the Fleet Wilma Hayes, sir!" Admiral Hayes was Marie Hayes's aunt, and right now Emma Shaw figured it was good to remind Captain Rahn about that since Marie's life hung in the balance. It would look awfully bad on his gleaming service record to have lost the boss's niece.

Captain Rahn just looked at her, then glanced over toward the terrorists. Emma looked at them, too. They honestly seemed confused by what was going on and she didn't blame them much.

As she turned her head, her eyes met Captain Rahn's. "I can see, Commander Shaw," he said, smiling at her with his perfect white teeth, "that as ranking Navy officer on the scene, you had the situation under control. So, carry on, Commander." He turned on his heel and walked off, shouting to the young Chinese lieutenant jg who'd come up commanding the SP's, "Fong, take your orders from Commander Shaw. Carry on."

She was tempted to stick her tongue out at him, but she didn't. And even though Ward Aldridge was a Marine and had date of commission on her, Emma Shaw was technically the ranking officer.

But Emma Shaw didn't quibble.

Instead, still holding a gun in each hand and, for some silly reason, very conscious of the fact she'd torn out the right leg of her panty hose, she shouted, "Mr. Fong, deploy your personnel to surround the enemy vehicles. On the double!"

"Aye, aye, ma'am! You heard the commander! Move it!"

Then she looked back at what was going on. Captain Rahn had stuck her with the duty in the event Marie got killed, so she—Emma Shaw—would get the blame.

Ward Aldridge was out of his desert cab, crouched behind it, his pistol aimed at no one in particular.

She had the conn, so she'd use it. "Unarmed personnel withdraw to the far side of the street. Move it!"

119

The GI's who'd helped stop the enemy vehicles started drifting away as told.

She looked at the man who held a full-size energy pistol to Marie Hayes's head. He shouted toward her, "Back off, bitch, or she gets it! I mean it!"

Emma Shaw stooped over and set down the energy rifle. Her pistol in both hands, she raised it slowly, deliberately, into a point shoulder position. Fong's people were fully deployed now, ringing the two vehicles. If a shootout started, aside from Marie getting killed, Ward Aldridge would probably buy a stray bullet, too.

Her pistol on line with the terrorist spokesman's head, Emma Shaw raised her voice and said, "If you surrender your hostage and your weapons, you will be turned over to the civilian authorities of Port Reno. Which, as we both know, means you'll be able to talk or bribe your way out of trouble. If you do not cooperate, I will assume that your hostage will die anyway. Therefore, I will shoot your ass right now." She didn't want to remind the terrorists that their hostage was the niece of Fleet Admiral Hayes, of whom they had more than likely heard. That was why she avoided using Marie's name, instead referring to her as the hostage. And, more to the point at the moment, since the terrorist spokesman had not yet responded, she didn't want him to realize she was bluffing. "What'll it be? An easy buy-out or dead? I don't have all night, fella."

Women's equality had come a long way in six hundred years, but there was still the possibility that someone in long hair, a skirt, and heels wasn't quite intimidating enough to make these guys release their hostage and drop their guns.

Her father and her brother had taught her that once the guns came out, talk was limited, if not nonexistent, so she said nothing else, just kept the muzzle of her gun as steady as she could.

The terrorist spokesman—he was thirty or so and had a face that belonged to the psychopathic axe murderer in a horror movie—shoved Marie Hayes away from him. She stood there for a second, shrugging her jacket back up onto her shoulders but not walking off.

"Civilian authorities?"

Emma Shaw still didn't move her gun. "My word as an officer and lady."

"Lay 'em down, guys! Do it!" The man bent over and set his energy pistol on the pavement, then raised his hands over his head.

Hesitantly, Marie started walking toward Emma Shaw.

The other terrorists started laying down their weapons as well.

Emma Shaw shouted, "Mr. Fong!"

"Yes, ma'am?"

"See to it that these individuals are properly disarmed and that they are turned over to the civilian authorities as I promised. Confiscate their weapons and any pertinent documents on their mission. And get them photographed so we can throw their pretty faces into the computer."

"Yes, ma'am!"

Marie was nearly even with Emma now, and Emma Shaw started to lower her pistol. Marie was shaking her head, "Ohh, Emma, I almost pissed in my panty hose."

Emma Shaw uncocked her weapon and called out to Ward Aldridge, "Captain Aldridge!"

"Yes, ma'am?"

"Please take over here."

"Yes, ma'am."

Then Emma Shaw holstered her weapon.

Marie Hayes, her voice a little shaky-sounding, said, "You look kinda green. But maybe it's just the neon

121

lights, huh?"

"Remember about your panty hose? Well, I did pee mine."

And she wanted to throw up.

Then the beeper on her belt started signaling, not the trilling sound this time but the buzzing sound. She was being called to duty.

She could throw up out the window of the car on the way back to the docks.

Her damp panty hose would have to wait a while.

Chapter Twenty-One

The armored personnel carriers hadn't moved for well over an hour and a half. Neither had Paul Rubenstein.

But men in arctic gear were now starting to emerge from the rear doors of both vehicles, heavily armed.

Presumably, commanders and technicians were still inside.

They would be running sensor scans, Paul Rubenstein theorized, for thermal register, sound emissions, radar, and the like.

And they had to be on to the fact that someone was waiting down in the defile, or they would not have sent men out but instead would have pursued the hoofprints in the snow leading off and away from the site. But they did not know exactly where, had no fixed position. For if they had, their vehicles would have been in motion and in pursuit. That they had not pursued the preponderance of hoofprints leading off toward the town, to which the rather curious Mary Ann had led John and Natalia, was a very bad sign.

The scenario was clear to Paul Rubenstein, but he hoped it was not that obvious to the enemy personnel.

Either John or Natalia had come back with horses, evidently not even a wagon judging by the marks in the snow. When whichever one of them it was spotted the armored carriers coming up, some of the horses were cut loose, giving tracks to follow. The other horses were taken into the defile.

Paul estimated that, at best, John or Natalia and those other horses were five hundred yards from the enemy personnel who were now fanning out into the snow.

Three of these men were clearly Land Pirates, as evidenced by their garish garb and more basic weaponry, their affiliation obvious. The other six were either Eden Defense Forces or Nazi, and he was beginning to think there was such a faint line separating the two that it was almost nonexistent. The six were better uniformed and better armed and, somehow, seemed to move with more evident precision and purpose.

From what he knew about their vehicles, the standard operating crew consisted of a commander who doubled as back-up driver, the driver who doubled as engineer/weapons controller, and the navigator, who also operated communications and sensors.

That meant that besides the nine men starting toward the defile, there were likely six more, three inside each vehicle.

The vehicles themselves possessed a long litany of weapons capabilities, from energy cannons to missiles and, it was theorized, gas diffusion as well. Their armor, as best he could understand it, was vastly better than the most sophisticated U.S., Soviet, or British armor of the late Twentieth Century.

Paul Rubenstein did not like this new world very much. Even after one hundred twenty-five years, the present was too much like the past. Only the players had changed. The world was on a war footing again, and what civilization there was seemed retrograde in the extreme.

For the past hour and a half, while his limbs were

124

gradually numbing with the cold, he had been considering his options. There were few.

John was a good enough marksman to take on nine heavily armed men with virtually any firearm, and much the same could be said for Natalia; but he was not. With the Steyr-Mannlicher SSG, he would have stood a good chance. With his Schmiesser, if the distance had been half what it was, he might have tried it. But he was close to being out of effective range for the 9mm Parabellums his submachine gun fired. If he'd had an assault rifle, it would have been iffy at best.

So, sniping was out.

Once he started something, whichever one of his friends was down in the defile could be counted on, of course, to assist, but timing might be critical.

The only option he had not ruled out was the direct method.

That involved getting inside one of the armored personnel carriers and taking it over. There were, after all, nine men outside, but only three men in each of the armored personnel carriers.

"What am I doing here?" Paul Rubenstein asked himself. And then he smiled, because he knew the answer to the question. . . .

Martin Zimmer said, "I am cold."

"No shit, Sherlock. Join the club. If you weren't such an animal, none of us would be here in the first place. How can you live with yourself?" Annie finally asked him.

"Look. You are my sister. I will not see any harm come to you. And even though you have chosen poorly for a husband, because this Rubenstein is your husband—despite the fact that he is Jewish—I will spare his life. If you cooperate, that is. Otherwise, I will not be responsible."

Annie looked at him and smiled, even though her cheeks were so cold it hurt to do so. "Give it a rest, Martin," she told him. . . .

Mary Ann looked about ready to pass out.

Natalia Tiemerovna's fingers were so cold she wondered if she would be able to successfully operate her weapons.

But she lay still, almost motionless.

She could hear the sounds of booted feet crunching through the snow, coming toward her.

Her mission was, thus far, a failure. She had a total of six horses, a half-dozen blankets, and five coats, these latter taken from the bodies of the men John had killed in the saloon.

By now, after all the time that had passed, many of the women freed from the Land Pirates would be suffering severely from exposure. And, it was always possible, with the armored personnel carriers positioned as they were, that Paul and Annie and the freed women would just stumble upon the enemy, into a disaster.

But she had another thought now. What if Paul and Annie were considerably closer than she had thought? What if even now they, too, were aware of the enemy vehicles?

Did she have an ally out there, perhaps ready to strike?

But what could be done? No weapon they possessed would have any effect against the APCs. The modest amount of explosives available would cripple one of the machines, but only if detonated against a tread or detonated from inside. . . .

* * *

126

Paul Rubenstein had one pound of the latest German plastique.

And he had a plan.

Chapter Twenty-Two

"It's a planned demonstration," Manfred Kohl said matter-of-factly. "We cannot get involved."

Men and women, looking for all the world perfectly normal except for their sixties-style mod clothing—Nehru jackets, Mao caps, bell-bottom trousers, miniskirts, boots—were moving through the street, carrying torches and placards. The signs dealt with such standard anti-Semitic propaganda themes as Jewish conspiracies, Jewish financial manipulation, Jewish anti-government sentiment, etc.

Michael Rourke remembered once, as a boy, seeing a KKK demonstration. He'd asked his father and mother why the men were dressed in robes and funny pointed hats. His mother had said, "Some people hate, and when they see other people who don't, they don't like it. They want to make the other people hate, too."

These people hated. These demonstrators hated whether the hatred was genuine or staged. The intent was the same.

They were trying to make other people hate, too.

Moving slowly because of his wounds but moving nonetheless, Michael Rourke turned off into the side street, flanked by Manfred Kohl and James Darkwood.

He had other work this night.

The satellite uplink had been made, the message sent,

and the business at hand was to get out of Eden City alive so he could fight what grew here, not stay and make some futile gesture—like running up to a demonstrator and pulling the picket sign from his hands, and tearing it up—and then die.

Eden Defense force personnel and police were everywhere tonight. . . .

As it turned out, Emma Shaw had the time to change her panty hose anyway. She had been waiting in Captain Edmund Rahn's outer office for nearly ten minutes.

At last, his secretary answered an intercom—Emma Shaw could not hear the conversation, hard as she tried—and then looked at her and said, "Captain Rahn will see you now, Commander Shaw."

"Thank you, Seaman," Emma told the woman.

She approached the door, knocked, heard the perfunctory "Come in," and entered.

Emma walked across the room and came to attention before Captain Rahn's desk.

He said and did nothing for several seconds, then at last, as if suddenly remembering she was standing there, he looked up for a split second and said, "As you were, Commander. Take a seat."

"Thank you, sir," she responded, then took the chair just opposite him, setting her hat in her lap. She had a terrific impulse to clear her throat and break the silence, but she didn't. She just waited.

After what seemed to her like an eternity but realistically was only a minute or so, Captain Rahn—he was terrific looking, she thought—set down his pen and looked up from the documents he'd been perusing. They were Intell printouts. She'd seen enough of them over the years to recognize them at a distance. "I've just received orders from Admiral Hayes, personally. By the way, you did well with that mess you caused in Port Reno. I'm willing to forget the incident ever happened."

"Thank you, sir," she said, not meaning it.

"Admiral Hayes has been in touch with Allied Intelligence HQ. It seems there's an extraction that needs handling just west of the rift valley. I assume you're familiar with Dr. John Thomas Rourke?"

In spite of herself, Emma Shaw laughed. "No disrespect, sir, but who isn't?"

"A few people in the upper echelons have known this for quite some time, but Dr. Rourke did not die, as the rumors went. . . ."

"What? I mean, sir—"

"Dr. Rourke was critically injured, as goes the story, but he did not die. Dr. Rourke and his near-legendary family, the very same people my great-great-great-great-grandfather, Admiral Rahn, worked with one hundred and twenty-five years ago, are alive—or at least they were a little less than twenty-four hours ago."

"But Dr. Rourke and the others would be—"

"No, Commander Shaw, they would not be old. They survived by means of cryogenic sleep. I understand, from Admiral Hayes who has seen Dr. Rourke personally, that he looks like a man in his late thirties. He is physically unchanged from photos taken of him at the conclusion of the War with the Soviet Union. The same goes for his family, with the exception of his wife who remains in cryogenic sleep, and a German officer who joined them. Dr. Rourke, his son, his daughter and her husband, and the Russian woman who served so valiantly with Dr. Rourke, Major Tiemerovna, are all out there. Well, not the son. He is working with Commander James Darkwood, whom I believe you know." She knew him all right, having graduated with him from the Academy. James Darkwood was one of her best friends in the world. "Commander Darkwood, as you may know, is on detached duty to Allied Intelligence. But, Dr. Rourke, his daughter, her husband, and Major Tiemerovna are on the west side of the rift valley. Without extraction, their situation is considered hopeless."

"Yes, sir," Emma Shaw said.

"This is not something I can order you to do. But, if you volunteer and can find a sufficient number of other volunteers to undertake the mission with you, you'll be entirely on your own. We will officially disavow this mission should you be shot down and killed or captured by the Eden Defense Forces. Aircraft are being readied now, all markings removed, added armament pods installed."

"If I get them out, sir, bring them back here?"

"If you succeed in your mission, Commander, you will return here to refuel, drop off any wounded, then fly immediately to Pearl Harbor, where you will receive further orders." Captain Rahn had been looking at everything but her face, as was his habit, not just with her but with everyone, when he did a preliminary mission briefing. But now he looked her straight in the eye. His eyes were so powerful she had to blink. "I envy you this opportunity, Commander Shaw. And, should you accept, I caution you that Dr. Rourke still holds the rank of brigadier general, that was conferred upon him at Mid-Wake by the president personally more than a century ago."

"Consider me volunteered, sir."

Captain Edmund Rahn stood up. Emma stood up, too. He walked around the desk, extended his right hand to her, and said, "Good luck, Commander."

"Thank you, sir."

She turned, starting to leave. And she wondered what she was getting herself into now.

As she stepped into the outer office, Captain Rahn's

secretary handed her a video packet marked, "Eyes Only."

She knew exactly what she was getting herself into—something that would probably turn out to be more trouble than she could imagine.

Chapter Twenty-Three

Paul Rubenstein had inched his way through the snow along the north side of the slope until he was within twenty yards of the nearest of the two APCs.

Time was running out.

At any second, he expected to hear gunfire from the defile, where all nine of the field party had disappeared.

The APCs, aside from their standard sensing equipment, were equipped with intruder alert systems. All he had to do was touch one of the units and the system would kick on.

In New York City in the wintertime, he used to get together with his friends occasionally and go out to the park. All of them would pretend they were kids again, which usually meant getting into a snowball fight by the end of things. He had been a pretty good hand with a snowball, even as a little boy. He pulled off his outer and inner gloves, his hands instantly starting to numb even more than they had been. He kept the gloves under his left upper arm, pressed against his torso to trap the warmth inside as long as he could.

As his hands dipped into the snow, there was stinging pain.

But he had a proper amount of snow. And it was good packing snow, nice and wet. He formed it into a sphere that, to the naked eye at least, looked as perfectly round as round could be.

There was no time to waste, because his hands couldn't take the cold much longer. He rose to his feet and launched the snowball toward the rear door of the APC nearest him, then ducked, waiting for the hoped for reaction.

As he got his gloves back on, his hands shaking with the cold, the hatch started to open. There would be men waiting just inside, he knew.

But he had his Schmiesser to his shoulder, ready.

And in his pocket was another ball, this of plastique, about a quarter pound's worth, with a detonator displayed prominently, imbedded into it. Only the detonator was disabled.

He trusted that the intended recipients of the ball of plastique would not realize that.

The hatch was halfway down now, about as far as prudent men would lower it.

He lowered his weapon, took the ball of German plastique explosives from his pocket, and lobbed it toward the doorway where the opening was.

If he missed, he had a second ball prepared. He had learned that from John a long time ago: Plan ahead.

But Paul Rubenstein did not miss, the ball of plastique explosives and the neutralized detonator disappearing inside the APC's hatchway.

Nothing happened for a second or so.

If the men inside were nervy, they'd take a second to inspect the ball, albeit from a distance.

If not . . . the doorway opened downward all the way, the three men who had been inside now outside, running, pulling coats on and holding weapons at the same time. Paul Rubenstein had the German MP-40 submachine gun back to his shoulder and he fired, hosing out three long bursts, taking out all three men.

Then Paul was up, running toward the hatchway of the

134

APC before the turret gun on the second machine could open fire on him.

Now, if he could only have enough time to switch detonators. . . .

Natalia Tiemerovna heard gunfire.

She anticipated Mary Ann's scream, so she smothered it with her gloved right hand as the girl opened her mouth to utter it.

She heard voices, the men with the boots that crunched snow, very close to her, shouting to each other in beautiful German that something had gone wrong.

Natalia certainly hoped . . . .

Paul Rubenstein didn't bother pulling the neutralized detonator but simply inserted the fresh one, then slapped the ball of plastic explosives against the bulkhead near a row of riveted armor plates. The second ball was already in his hand as he moved forward, and Paul stuck it to the bulkhead near the hydraulic lines for the brakes. He set the timer.

And then he started aft, toward the open doorway.

The turret gun on the APC beside him was already firing, blue-white bolts of electrical energy cutting furrows into the snow just outside the doorway, far enough away not to hit the APC itself.

Paul Rubenstein dodged right, counting seconds as he ran. Fifteen seconds remained.

Now fourteen.

He jumped from the ramp and into the snow, a bolt from the energy weapon mounted on the second APC's turret just missing him, but a shower of partially vaporized snow falling around him, drenching him.

He threw himself beside the tread at the APC's left rear.

Nine seconds.

He could hear the transmission of the second APC, the vehicle starting into motion.

If the commander of the second machine were really smart, he'd guess.

Paul hoped the man wasn't that smart.

Four seconds. Paul burrowed as deeply as he could into the snow, almost but not quite in contact with the tread.

Three. If he had calculated the strength of the vehicle incorrectly, he would be dead.

Two.

Paul Rubenstein's hands were over his ears and his submachine gun was protected beneath his body.

The blast came, not loud at all to begin with, then peaking in volume with a screech, the ground shaking, the sounds of metal groaning, tearing, the APC beside which he'd taken shelter lurching sideways and away from him as he watched.

And then there was a second explosion, and Paul Rubenstein knew that what he'd done had worked, turning the armored personnel carrier into a gigantic fragmentation bomb to destroy the second identical vehicle.

Now all he had to worry about were the nine men armed and afoot in the defile.

Chapter Twenty-Four

Natalia Tiemerovna was up, moving, hissing to Mary Ann under her breath, "Stay here with the horses. Do as I say or you will be in trouble!" She was taking advantage of the girl and she knew it, capitalizing on Mary Ann's low self-esteem, but there was no time to do otherwise.

Natalia ran obliquely along the wall of the defile, so she would not run right into the men who searched for her. Whatever had happened, from the sound of the explosions, it had to have affected their vehicles.

So they would be returning to the vehicles. Natalia reached the height of the defile, staying just below its crest so she would not silhouette herself against the skyline. The night was bright.

She ran into a stand of scrub pine, her short-barreled assault rifle ready, her coat open at the chest so she could access her suppressor-fitted pistol should the need arise.

And it did.

As she cut through the trees, she saw the rear edge of the party of searchers, counting at least nine men, running toward a descending fireball and a twisted pile of blackened wreckage.

She saw a figure moving from the far side of the wreckage.

The only way she could tell it was Paul was because Annie was back in skirts.

Natalia flung herself down into the snow, letting the as-

137

sault rifle fall across her back, her right hand ripping the suppressor-fitted Walter PPK/S from the shoulder holster, her right thumb—she had her outer gloves off—flicking up the safety into the fire position.

She thumbed back the hammer, both elbows steady in the snowy ground, holding her breath, letting a little of it go, then starting the trigger squeeze. With any luck she could take out two of them before they realized where she was shooting from. . . .

Paul Rubenstein, his ears ringing so loudly that he couldn't have heard a third explosion if there had been one, had the Schmiesser to his right shoulder, firing controlled three round bursts. He put down two of the nine men, one of them a Land Pirate, before the others started returning fire.

And as they returned fire, he threw himself behind the cover of the left side of the APC.

Energy pulses pinged off the armor work, electrical charges flickering across the hull. . . .

Natalia had one man down, and was squeezing the trigger on the second, when a third man—she had him at the edge of her peripheral vision—started to turn around. She let the second man live for a moment longer, swung her pistol to the man who was turning around, and put a bullet into his throat.

His energy weapon discharged into the sky, a blue lightning bolt arcing upward.

Natalia swung her weapon back to her original target.

Paul had swapped shots with some of the men, but she didn't know why he wasn't firing still, unless, of course he'd been hit. She finished the trigger squeeze and the man who'd been her original second target became her third, grabbing for his left ear as the bullet struck.

138

She was pushing her luck and she knew it. Dropping the safety on the American Walter, she stuffed the longish combination of pistol and suppressor into an outside pocket of her parka. Grabbing for her assault rifle, she rose to her feet and ran back into the trees.

An energy pulse impacted a tree about a meter from her, engulfing the trunk with fire, the sapling pine toppling over and nearly falling on her. She dodged right.

There was standard submachine gun fire now from behind her. . . .

Paul Rubenstein emerged from the far end of the demolished second APC, already firing.

He cut down one man, a Land Pirate, as the man was firing toward the trees.

John or Natalia was out there, Rubenstein bet with himself.

He charged forward, firing into the remaining three men who were running toward where the defile began.

Paul couldn't hear anything at all, and there was a dull roar in his ears. It would pass, he hoped. But, for the moment, he was deaf.

The three men were at the crest of the defile.

As Paul brought his weapon to his shoulder, he caught a flash of movement to his right and wheeled about toward it.

Natalia.

She had the short-barreled assault rifle she carried up to her shoulder, firing it.

Paul fired.

The three men running for the defile started to fall.

And immediately, especially since he had just destroyed the best transportation they could ask for, the reality of beating the cold before the women died of exposure washed over him like the sounds of the waves crashing in his still-ringing ears.

139

Chapter Twenty-Five

It was nearly dawn, and John Rourke guided the big grey to the height of a rise.

In the valley below, there was a farmhouse.

The coordinates on the map he had memorized, his compass bearings, and a gut feeling told him he had reached the safe house.

It was still well over a mile away, and there was no sign of a fire from the house's crude stone chimney. If the Allied agents Hilda, Dan, and Margie, were not there, at least there should be a radio for making a satellite uplink and contact with Allied Intelligence Headquarters. But that would take even more time.

His hopes rested on the barn.

The weathered grey clapboard structure, it's roof half collapsed, was big enough to house several vehicles. And the Allied agents had said there would be transportation available for however many personnel he brought out of the Land Pirates' stronghold with him.

He hoped it was there.

The night had been long and cold for him, and he knew it had been worse for Paul and Annie and the freed women. Natalia would have long since reached them, and with ten horses used wisely, they would have made better time and might be close to the town again—those seven buildings in the middle of nowhere where he'd had the gunfight with Mary Ann's "old man" and company.

He urged his mount ahead, telling both animals, as if they could understand him, "There's gonna be the best-tasting feed you guys ever had, and I'll rub you both down and you'll be warm. I promise."

John Rourke hoped he was right. . . .

Emma Shaw zipped into her flight suit, then slung her shoulder holster into position. The Lancer 2570 A2-C was cleaned and freshly loaded. She strapped her knife to the outside of her right calf, a Bowie pattern with a six-inch blade made from five-sixteenths stainless stock. Anything longer could have interfered with movement, and the thickness of the stock in conjunction with the short length of the blade made for a combination that was virtually unbreakable in human hands.

Emma looked into the mirror, picked up her spare brush, and ran it through her hair several times. Then she caught her hair up almost at the crown of her head with a rubber band, which had a bead at either end, winding it around twice so it would stay put under her helmet.

It looked really sexy just to make a toss of the head and pull on the helmet, but when she took it off, she had a head full of knots. This way, with a ponytail to start with, she at least had a fighting chance.

She grabbed up her helmet and her flight bag, which had already been checked. A survival kit, spare ammunition for her pistol, marker flares, and such were right where they should be, along with a change of underwear and a sweater.

She shrugged into her A-2, then took a final look at what had been her home for the last one hundred eighty-seven days. Maybe she'd be back here, and maybe she wouldn't. But she hoped Marie Hayes or somebody wouldn't be packing up her stuff and sending it back to

Honolulu to two cops with the last name of Shaw, in the custody of some Lieutenant jg in a dress uniform with a note signed by the President of the United States. She loved the American flag, but not enough to wear it. . . .

Michael Rourke's body was about at shut-down level by the time the antique V-stol aircraft settled on the field fifty or so miles south of Eden City.

Manfred Kohl, who seemed to be the least happy man Michael Rourke had ever met, commented dryly, "You realize that to get under Eden air defense sensors is very risky and we might all be killed if they fire a missile at us."

James Darkwood looked at Michael, then at Kohl. "Manfred, you know I like you . . . that you're my best friend in the whole world, right?"

"This is true."

"Right. But why the hell do you have to be so depressing all the time, Manfred? Gee-whiz!" James Darkwood then spoke into his radio, saying, "This is Orphan, Fairy Godmother. We're on our way. Acknowledge. Over."

Michael Rourke could barely hear the low frequency response coming back through Darkwood's radio, but he didn't care. He grabbed up the shotgun-sized grenade launcher he'd been carrying ever since they got into the car to leave Eden — he'd had no intention of being taken alive — and started walking onto the field. Aboard the aircraft, he told himself, he could sleep. . . .

There was clear evidence of a fight. That was certain.

Croenberg said, "Herr Doctor, I tried my best. But the young Rourke, I am afraid, was able to overpower me. One of the main floor guards was found in the alley beside our building. He was given an injection and has not

142

yet been revived by our doctors. But it is safe to assume young Rourke escaped. And I am also afraid," Croenberg continued, "that our beloved Martin has fallen into enemy hands."

Deitrich Zimmer looked into Croenberg's eyes. He could not read them, but then Croenberg was an accomplished man, and lying might be one of his accomplishments. . . .

John Rourke swung down out of the miserable excuse for a saddle, his tailbone hurting him.

He drew both Scoremasters from his belt.

The door to the farmhouse opened.

Her grey eyes scowling, Hilda stepped out so rapidly that John Rourke nearly shot her to death.

"I understand that you have Martin." Her German accent was showing a little. "I also have just been notified that the Americans are sending out a group of Interceptors to pick you up and then find the rest of your party. It is a pity, really, because I wanted to see Martin."

John Rourke didn't put away his guns, and wouldn't until he saw the inside of the house and made certain everything was as it should be. But he smiled as he told Hilda, "If you've seen my face, you've seen Martin Zimmer's face. Got anything hot I can consume after I take care of the horses?"

Chapter Twenty-Six

She flew into the sun.

The first time she'd been up at the controls of an aircraft—despite the fact she had a senior pilot instructor with her—the beauty of what she saw struck her. It hadn't left her in all the years since.

Aviation was lost to the United States while she survived only beneath the Pacific at Mid-Wake. One of the first—if not *the* first—citizens of Mid-Wake to be aboard an aircraft in five centuries was the heroic Captain Jason Darkwood, later Admiral of the Fleet. Mid-Wake's aviation program began in earnest, with the aid of New Germany, in the decade immediately following the conclusion of the war.

Almost immediately after the Underground City in the Urals was taken by Dr. Rourke and the Allied armies, and Jason Darkwood led his famous raid against the Soviet Undersea Complex, the people of Mid-Wake began returning to the surface.

Some made what later proved to be a colossal error, going to what had been the United States and was now Eden. Almost from the beginning, Eden had became the antithesis of its name, not a paradise but a boot camp for hell instead.

But other citizens of Mid-Wake reestablished an American presence in the Hawaiian Islands. The islands had changed considerably during the five centuries they were uninhabited. With the global climate change, temperatures ranged from below freezing in the winter to the mid to upper eighties on the Fahrenheit scale during high summer. Topography had changed as well. Hawaii's several volcanoes had been particularly active during those five hundred years, and sea levels rose and fell and rose again. No one who had known the islands during the Twentieth Century would have recognized them now. They were still as close to paradise on earth as man could attain, but of a different sort . . . less fragile. Orchids still grew, but the snow in the high mountains was so reliably deep that skiing had become one of the islands' favorite pastimes.

In the one hundred twenty-five years since the end of the war, the United States had once again become a surface power and was now at parity with New Germany in air power. And, of course, the United States had the greatest navy in the world.

New Germany possessed a token navy at best but had the second largest-standing army, second only to Eden. Australia had a modestly sized but well-respected air force and navy. Eden's navy was small but wonderfully well equipped.

But to think that for centuries no Americans had flown was almost incomprehensible to her. To Emma Shaw, flying was as much a part of life as breathing. And the Interceptor she flew was the finest aircraft of its type in the world.

The Interceptor was based on the concept behind the much-revered prewar SR-71, an aircraft capable of high altitude flight and ultra high speed, which was nonetheless enormously handleable. Archaeologists kept finding things all over the world, relics from Before The Night Of The War. If, somehow, an archeological team ever dug up an SR-71, she'd almost kill to fly it.

145

But the Interceptor was better. It could do Mach 7 if it had to yet had the ability to convert to V-stol operation, so it could land on a postage stamp and take off from the roof of a building. The Interceptor had the capacity to carry twelve persons plus a two-man crew (or equivalent cargo weight) and no one quite knew just how high it would fly if pushed. Someday she wanted to do that. Its variable swept-wing-forward leading canard design was the ultimate best. To fly a plane in combat, she knew, it was imperative to think of that aircraft as the best there was. But she truly believed it.

There was considerable talk of a space program as a cooperative effort between members of the Trans-Global Alliance, but nothing would happen with that until the crisis with Eden was resolved.

And Emma grew ever more convinced that would only be resolved with a war.

Unlike the SR-71, the Interceptor was a battle plane. The SR-71, according to what she had read, did not carry armament because it outflew its attackers, but missiles, flew much faster these days. And, aside from missiles on the weapons pods, there were forward and aft firing electric mini-guns.

Emma looked to the right and left, her wingmen just where they should be. The volunteers to fly the three aircraft in and extract the Rourke party were just whom she thought they would be—Marie Hayes and Wally Theodore. Wally was out of the Academy only two years but was naturally gifted as a flyer.

Marie was tops as well.

Between the three aircraft, since none had a copilot/navigator aboard, they could carry thirty-nine passengers and gear. According to the Intell tapes she'd viewed and the printouts she'd seen, there were twenty-four female prisoners rescued from the hands of the Land Pi-

146

rates, John Rourke, his daughter and her husband, Major Tiemerovna, and an unnamed male prisoner.

She wondered if the man were the leader of the Land Pirates or perhaps one of the Nazi advisors to the Eden Forces. Whoever it was, taking any sort of Eden official prisoner was a political hot potato.

And what was the second half of her mission, once she got in, made the pickup, and got out?

Maybe taking Dr. Rourke to Hawaii or Mid-Wake to meet with Admiral Hayes?

Emma Shaw dwelt on the idea of John Rourke.

Meeting him was like meeting . . . she didn't know whom, but perhaps George Washington was the closest. He was a living legend, homage to John Rourke and the common language of English, all that the United States and Eden had in common these days.

John Rourke's face was on both nations' currency, postage, in every history textbook.

Sometimes, being a woman was a pain. Male officers didn't have to worry about panty hose to go with dress uniforms, artfully arranging hair so it looked in regs, things like that. Yet sometimes, when it came to meeting a man like Dr. General John Thomas Rourke, being a woman was a pure delight.

He had to be the sexiest man in human history, or at least she hoped so, because otherwise she'd be terribly disappointed. . . .

Michael Rourke slept through the plane ride, consumed a hot meal while he was debriefed by Allied Intelligence personnel in New Caracas, then had his wounds re-dressed, showered, and changed into German Battle Dress Utilities.

Ten minutes later, a selection of weapons flown up

147

from New Germany was shown to him. Knowing his fondness for what he and the rest of The Family individually and collectively considered "real guns," these were reproductions of classic Twentieth Century small arms manufactured in Hawaii by Lancer Corporation.

He'd seen Lancer repros before going to Eden and was impressed, the exactness of detail, right down to metallurgy, markings, and of course, all functional characteristics beyond reproduction more like forgery of the highest order. Somewhere on each piece, artfully hidden, was the Lancer name and corporate logo, a knight on horseback carrying a lance. This was out of necessity.

Archaeologists were constantly uncovering relics from the pre-war civilization, and the few antique arms recovered fetched enormous prices in the collector market. To prevent the Lancer guns from being represented as the original articles, they bore their microscopic markings.

Michael Rourke's own weapons, among those his two Beretta pistols, were in the custody of his family and he was certain he would have them back as soon as he and The Family were reunited. A German ordinance officer had offered him what he later found out was a year's salary for just one of the Beretta 92Fs, but he refused.

From among the Lancer reproductions, he selected a gun with which he had always been fascinated. It was ultimately practical for his use. The gun was an identical duplicate of the one-time widely available and subsequently banned-for-importation 9mm Parabellum Uzi carbine. In his father's firearms reference library and videos, he'd seen the Uzi carbine as rugged, durable, and utilitarian, features he found irresistible.

Now he had one, a duplicate of the "Type B," the last model imported in the declining years of the Twentieth

148

Century before misguided do-gooder lawmakers labeled various inanimate objects as evil and proscribed their importation.

There were submachine guns available to him, but although selective fire weapons were useful at times, he liked the longer barrel of the semi-automatic carbine. With a variety of magazines, ranging from the short twenty-rounders to thirty-two rounds in length, he felt he was adequately armed for the trip to Hawaii should unforeseen trouble arise.

Lancer also made identical duplicate ammunition, based on the Federal Cartridge ammunition his family had always used. He laid up a supply of this as well, having the bulk of the 115-grain jacketed hollow points and most of the magazines sent to the aircraft he would soon be boarding, keeping one primary magazine and two spares with him. An issue German bayonet would do until he had his own knife back.

Before boarding the aircraft, he met again with the agents from Allied Intelligence who had briefed him, a man in his fifties with an open, smiling face and a woman in her thirties. She didn't seem to know how to smile properly but was otherwise pleasant enough, although rather plain.

New Caracas was principally a German Air Base, with a small town grown up around it. They met in one of the pilot ready rooms.

The woman closed the door.

Michael sat down, his legs still paining him a little and the wound in his side bothering him as well. But he was mainly tired.

The woman said, "Herr Rourke, I must commend you for the intelligence coup you have achieved. The data concerning the invasion of Hawaii and the attack on Pearl Harbor seems to check out. But we have no indication how soon the attack is to be launched. Can you remember nothing else?"

"There was nothing else. When my sister and I were growing up in The Retreat, I used to play memory games with myself. I've always been able to memorize things rather easily. If there were any other data, I would have remembered it and told you when I was debriefed."

The smiling-faced man asked, "Then what is your impression? Just the mood of the briefing you were privy to. What do you think their timetable might be? If you had to guess, I mean."

"Does this mean I have to guess?" Michael asked in return, smiling.

The woman paced the room, hands thrust into the pockets of her slacks. "Something subliminal, Herr Rourke, might seem like mere supposition to you but might be a starting point for us to utilize while we attempt to judge what their timetable might be."

Michael considered that, seeing no harm in giving a guess, but seeing little potential good in it, either. "Fine," he said at last, mentally shrugging. "And this is based on nothing but my gut level reaction, all right?"

"That is what we want, Herr Rourke," the smiling man said, nodding cheerfully.

"I'd say within two weeks at the most, but more likely a week."

"Why?" The woman stopped pacing and stared at him abruptly.

"It was—" He thought about it and really didn't know why. At last he said, "Just vibes."

"Vibes, Herr Rourke?" She looked as if she did not understand his use of the word, and he realized she probably didn't.

"Just a feeling, okay?"

150

"A feeling. Good!" She nodded her head and resumed her pacing of the room, between him and the door.

"If you should remember anything else," the man said, "well, of course—" And he smiled good-naturedly.

"Of course," Michael told him.

The woman opened the door.

Michael Rourke guessed that meant it was time to leave. But he didn't stand up yet. There was a question he wanted answered. "What about my people?"

The woman replied. "Your memory is better than mine. I was so concerned with asking you questions that I forgot to tell you something." She looked at her wrist and the timepiece there, rather large for a woman now that Michael noticed it. "In approximately eight minutes, three United States Interceptor long-range fighter transports should be making first contact with the Allied agents whom you encountered in the Wildlands. After that, it is a matter of searching the area in which your family was operating. There are no reports that the Interceptors were picked up on Eden defense systems."

That sounded good, Michael thought. On impulse, he asked the woman, "Do you know the name of the officer commanding the mission? I mean, I don't know anybody at Mid-Wake or in Hawaii, but I'm just kind of curious."

The woman looked up at the ready room's ceiling, as though she were consulting a notepad. Then she looked back at him. "The mission is being handled by a United States Naval officer. A Commander Shaw."

"Well, I hope this Shaw's a good guy."

"I am sure, Herr Rourke, that our American allies would have sent the best pilot they had available to head up the mission."

Michael nodded and stood up. The smiling man offered his hand and Michael took it.

151

The woman opened the door. "Have a safe flight. Until we meet again, then."

Michael walked past her, echoing, "Until we meet again."

Chapter Twenty-Seven

He saw to the horses first, as he'd promised, not trusting Hilda or either of the two others to do as thorough a job of rubbing down the animals as was required. And he fed and watered them, seeing to it that their shelter was adequate at least.

Then he washed his hands and face, sat down, and consumed two packets of field rations and a glass of whiskey.

Then he slept.

By the black face of the Rolex on his left wrist, he had slept for an hour and twelve minutes when Hilda awakened him. "I have just received a transponder signal. The planes are coming, Herr Doctor."

"Good."

John Rourke sat up. He rubbed his hands over his eyes.

"Will you want those awful blankets again?" Hilda asked him.

He touched Hilda's forearm. "I think not. Thank you." What he wanted was a shower but there were no facilities, and had there been, there was no time.

He crossed the snow to the little outhouse, watching for the first sign of the aircraft as they came overhead. Nothing yet. He entered the little outhouse. It was cold enough that the place didn't smell. There was no need to defecate. He'd done that less than six hours ago, during one of the periods while he'd rested the horses. But he urinated.

As he started to close the fly of his pants, he heard three sonic booms, one after the other.

When he stepped from the outhouse, he saw three matte black aircraft, two just coming over the horizon and the third landing in V-stol mode.

She touched down, Marie Hayes and Wally Theodore flying a low subsonic patrolling pattern that would cover a radius of fifty miles in all directions. If any Eden tanks or APCs or Land Pirate fortresses were around, Marie and Wally would put them away.

Interceptors did not have energy cannons, simply because of the weight, but the missiles on their pods could kill or cripple any Eden armor made — she hoped. At least that was what the instruction booklet that came with the missiles said.

She locked down, leaving her engines running, using the excuse of touchdown to unbuckle and stand up. Interceptors had comfortable seats, but nothing was comfortable to sit in without moving. Emma could just as easily have popped her portside hatch remotely, but she didn't, choosing instead to walk back along the length of the fuselage as she removed her helmet and shook her ponytail free.

She hit the manual controls and the hatch started to open.

There was a man walking toward her, a pack on his back, pistols in his belt. He wore nothing more than a heavy military sweater, slacks, and combat boots.

154

He was tall.

He was lean, but from the way he moved he was also well muscled and athletic. His face was thin, too, with not an ounce of fat on it, the bone structure solid and strong. His mouth was wide, with lines at the corners that looked like enormous dimples as the sides turned down.

His hair was dark brown with a little bit of grey, in patches, which became more noticeable the nearer he got. His hairline was strong, although his forehead was high. He looked like he was normally clean shaven but wasn't now.

She could not see his eyes. Sunlight glinted on the snow and he wore old-style aviator-type sunglasses, presumably against the glare.

He looked handsomer than he did in all his pictures, in all the statues.

This was John Rourke. . . .

John Thomas Rourke neared the fuselage door.

There was a tall, thin, beautiful woman with auburn hair and incredibly long legs standing in the open doorway.

He reminded himself that this was the future, so to speak, and it was wholly possible for a woman to be the copilot or navigator on a military fighter aircraft. Women generally had better reflexes than men and made excellent pilots.

He started to shrug out of his pack as he walked, catching it up under his arm as he neared the doorway, then throwing it inside as the woman looked down and said rather formally, "General Rourke, this is a true privilege."

155

He looked up at her, saying, "If you've gotta call me anything besides John, Dr. Rourke's better. Okay? But I really prefer John." She wore no rank or unit insignia, so he fell back on, And you're Miss—?

"I'm Commander Emma Shaw, sir. I'll reiterate. This is a genuine pleasure, sir."

She had a pretty voice, a nice soft alto, definitely feminine but with a good touch of authority to it.

As he started to climb aboard—she reached out a hand and he took it—Rourke asked, "Can I see the pilot, Commander? We have to make some time."

She pulled back and he was inside, standing face to face with her. She had pretty grey-green eyes, but they weren't smiling. "Sir, I hope you are not displeased, but I am the pilot. In fact, I'm the mission commander."

John Rourke started to laugh.

Now the pretty eyes looked downright hard.

He shook his head, saying, "No, Commander, I'm not laughing at you. I'm laughing at me. I must look pretty stupid with egg all over my face. Or do they still use that expression?"

"We still use it, sir." And now the eyes smiled, the lips smiled, the whole face smiled, in fact. She was very pretty in a comfortable sort of way. "And, yes, sir, I do see a little egg there, now that you mention it."

Rourke extended his right hand to her, saying, "How about John, okay?"

"Emma."

"Emma. I think I can guide you to the others. You have medical supplies, food, warm clothing aboard?"

"Your son—John, your son contacted the Navy through Allied Intelligence. We're fully—"

156

"Michael's all right?"

She smiled, nodding and saying, "As far as I know, sir. But I'm fully briefed. Except for the identity of your prisoner."

Good for Michael, John Rourke thought, alive and keeping Martin Zimmer in the bag. Or perhaps the information was only withheld from her. There was no way to tell. John Rourke decided that it was the right moment to show some trust. He told Commander Emma Shaw, "Our prisoner is Martin Zimmer. He's the leader of Eden, and he was born exactly a hundred and twenty-five years ago, even though he's only thirty. He looks like me but more like my son. Michael was impersonating him."

"Holy shit, sir."

"Precisely, Commander," John Rourke told her. "Precisely. Now, maybe we should get airborne and find the rest of the people you're supposed to rescue. Hopefully, the cold will be their only problem."

She looked at him hard and even, saying, "Whatever the problem, sir, short of the entire Eden Air Force, you don't have anything to worry about. We got in, we'll get 'em, and we'll get out. Then I fly you and your family and the freed female prisoners to my ship, which is anchored off Port Reno, Nevada, drop off the freed prisoners, then fly you and whomever else you direct to come along to Hawaii."

"Hawaii?"

"Your guess is as good as mine, sir."

"How old are you?"

"What, sir?"

"Please," Rourke insisted.

"Thirty, sir."

"Please stop calling me 'sir,' because I was born over

157

six and a half centuries ago and feel old enough, okay?"

She laughed.

Chapter Twenty-Eight

Deitrich Zimmer had several choices.

The segmented geodesic dome above him sheltered an array of plants, ranging from those once found in abundance in tropical rain forests to those of the northern tundra. The plants were coming back, but not yet as before. He had never seen "before," but he had read, watched tapes, and studied all he could about them. He had always considered himself a Socratic man.

Sometimes, his greatest lament was that life was not long enough to learn everything. If only it had been possible to acquire knowledge while he'd taken cryogenic sleep. He could have known all there was to learn of human knowledge, but then he still would have been merely scratching the surface.

There was so much yet to learn.

He chose the tropical rain forest segment of this domed paradise. As he walked in the rooftop garden, he considered his alternatives. This was a moment of history, and whatever decision he made would echo through the vaults of the future. So that decision must be a good one, the very best.

Martin was, most likely, still a prisoner of the Rourke family. John Rourke would not kill his own son, of course, and even if he entertained the thought, Martin would be safe as long as Sarah Rourke hovered between life and death and the only person who could free her was Deitrich Zimmer. Sooner or later, John Rourke would get word to him, suggesting a trade of sorts, Martin in exchange for certain services.

So Deitrich Zimmer dismissed thoughts of Martin, although he could not dismiss the anxiety he felt. Because Martin was his son, regardless of whose loins he sprang from.

He considered the immediately pressing matter of the attack on the United States fleet at Pearl Harbor.

The great preponderance of United States sea and air power was to be found at Pearl Harbor. Michael Rourke had sat through a briefing, so presumably Allied Intelligence knew of the plan or soon would, in as much detail as was divulged.

Four choices, then, lay before him.

He could cancel the attack, postpone the attack, accelerate the attack's timetable, or go ahead as planned with the attack's existing timetable.

If he went ahead as planned, the Trans Global Alliance would never have sufficient time to prepare, regardless of knowing that the attack was coming.

And so much was already in motion to turn plans and contingencies into reality.

He paused, considering a hibiscus.

Lovely.

What about Croenberg?

The fight with Michael Rourke in Martin's suite—there was something odd about it. Deitrich Zimmer had survived all these years by never trusting anyone or anything. And just because they shared similar political, philosophical, and racial beliefs didn't mean he trusted Croenberg and this current crop of SS. Croenberg's people knew nothing of science and reality.

More than a year ago, Croenberg had enthused wildly

over the absurd pseudoscience that was popular within the Third Reich. The universe, Croenberg said, was made of fire and ice, and only the earth combined the two.

But did Croenberg believe this nonsense, or was he merely trying to disarm fears for his — Croenberg's — intellectual abilities?

Once the war was begun and had its own momentum, the time would be right to cleanse the party of persons he did not trust, persons who might work against Martin's inherent superiority.

Croenberg and his fellows had a fondness for the history of the Third Reich. Deitrich Zimmer wondered how well they remembered The Night Of The Long Knives in 1934, when Hitler rid himself of his brownshirts.

Perhaps Croenberg recalled it all too well.

Perhaps Croenberg sought to prevent history from repeating itself, by destroying his Führer before he could destroy him. If that were the case, then Croenberg and his entire SS were potentially deadly enemies, more to be reckoned with than the military forces of the Trans-Global Alliance that stood against Eden's destiny.

There was time, because the beginning of the war would consume all energies, consume all minds.

Deitrich Zimmer walked on, entering the segment where there was desert plant life. A barrel cactus flowered amid the sand. The air here was so dry compared to the humidity of the rain forest segment that his sinuses began to react.

He would leave the dome and return to Martin's suite. There was to be a meeting with Croenberg and the others.

Deitrich Zimmer's decisions were made — about the attack on Pearl Harbor, about Croenberg's eventual fate, and even about what he would do when John Rourke presented him with the inevitable offer.

161

He would accept.

John Rourke's honor would not allow that a truce be violated. Martin would be safe for the moment and Rourke would find even greater sorrow, because his wife would be restored to him but her mind would be gone. While extracting the bullet, Zimmer would see to that. From the medical records he had studied of the incident, with his skill and his instruments he could extract the bullet, leaving Sarah Rourke unimpaired and fully restored.

But as he removed the bullet, it would be very easy to allow his instruments to slip, a bit this way, a bit that way.

Deitrich Zimmer would see to that. What better punishment than to give John Rourke a drooling imbecile to care for while the world around him collapsed into defeat for everything in which he believed!

He had won against John Rourke one hundred twenty-five years ago, and he would win against him now again.

Life could be greater punishment than death, and so it would be with John Rourke. When this war was won, let Rourke live, lock him away with a wife without a mind, let his mind and all he was dissolve to dust.

That was true revenge.

Chapter Twenty-Nine

"I know this is a silly question, Dr. Rourke, but how does it feel to be you? I mean—"

John Rourke was more interested in studying the cockpit of the Interceptor or possibly in some sleep. But instead he was studying the terrain zipping by beneath them. The last thing he wanted to talk about with this young woman was himself. But he tried to be polite and truthful with her. "I just happened to be in the right place at the right time . . . or the wrong place at the wrong time, depending on one's perspective, Commander."

"Please . . . Emma."

He'd all but given up on trying to get her to call him by his first name. "Emma," Rourke repeated.

"But, I mean, you must be aware of the pivotal role you played. Without you, at least according to what the history books and the movies all say—"

"Movies," Rourke repeated.

"Haven't you seen Lance whats-it play you? I mean, even though the film was made in Eden and it's loaded with propaganda . . . I mean, it was terrific."

"What sort of propaganda?"

She didn't answer for a moment.

"What sort of propaganda?" Rourke asked again.

She looked at him and smiled a little sheepishly. "I thought you'd seen the thing. Well," she began again, "they have you spouting off a lot of anti-Semitic stuff. . . ."

"What?"

"And your son-in-law, Paul Rubenstein . . . In the movie, he came from Jewish grandparents but disowned them, and what brought the two of you together was—"

"Don't tell me," Rourke groaned.

"But don't worry," Emma Shaw said brightly. "There's a movie in production in Hawaii right now with Brad Lang—he's a real hunk and he's a pretty good actor. . . ." She must have realized what she'd just said, Rourke surmised, because what he could see of her cheeks past the outline of her helmet seemed to be reddening in a blush. He found that sweet, somehow. "Anyway," she went on, "I was reading that they wanted to film on location, but Eden wouldn't allow it unless the government had editorial control of the script. They'd got this terrific guy to play Rubenstein, I understand. He's an unknown, but they auditioned more than a hundred young actors until they found just the right one. Say, wouldn't they owe you money . . . I mean, making a film about your life and everything?"

"Probably public domain. And, although some time I'm sure I'll need to find a way of making money again, at the moment I have no need for it."

She turned her head and looked at him. "You don't know?"

"Don't know what?" Rourke asked her.

She started to laugh. "It was in the Intell stuff I went through before the mission. You're still on the roll of officers, as a brigadier general. That means they must owe you—"

Rourke laughed. "That was honorary, just something done at the time. I never took it seriously. I wore a uniform exactly once, the night—"

164

Memories of that night, the night Akiro Kurinami and Elaine Halversen celebrated their wedding, the last night he'd seen Sarah alive, flooded back to him. He looked away from this talkative woman and studied the ground even more intently.

If he had been a little quicker, hadn't let Sarah go to the clinic alone, hadn't . . .

"What did I say?" Emma Shaw asked him.

"The only time I wore my uniform was the night my son—now Martin Zimmer—was born, my wife was shot in the head, and I wound up wearing quite a bit of my clinic's construction materials all over me and went into a coma that I didn't awaken from for one hundred and twenty-five years. They going to put that in the movie? How I screwed up?"

He still didn't look at her and Emma was silent for a moment. John Rourke was beginning to realize that silence on this woman's part was exceedingly rare, so he didn't attempt to break it. As he expected, she did. "I did a term paper on you once. That was when the official version was that you and your family were all dead. As far as I understood it, your clinic was firebombed and you went inside to rescue people and were trapped in the debris from an explosion."

"That's more or less the way it happened, except I should have been there earlier and none of it—"

"I read that a heavily armed force of Nazi commandoes was responsible for it. What could one man have done?"

They were passing over the seven buildings that were the miserable excuse for a town, where John Rourke had shot it out with Mary Ann's "old man" and a number of the fellow's associates.

"I could have made a difference, Bear south from here, along that ridge line. Keep that to your right."

165

She didn't say anything for a moment, cleared her throat, then brought her radio up to her mouth. "Do not acknowledge this transmission by radio. This is Aloha Leader." She recited compass bearings, then, "Prepare to enter into Mode Beta, I say again, Mode Beta, on my mark. Four. Three." Her hands seemed to fly more rapidly over the Interceptor's controls than the plane itself flew over the rugged terrain beneath them. "Two. One. Mark." She pulled the Velcro tab and the mouthpiece for her radio fell away as she started the machine into a steep bank, the portside wing tipping downward, the aircraft's attitude nearly ninety degrees to the hard deck. "Hold on, Dr. Rourke. We're going right up one of Eden Defense Command's sensor alleys for the next—" she consulted her instruments, "make that ninety-four seconds. We'll be flying in a manner that will seem rather erratic to you, I'm afraid."

As all the blood started moving to the left side of his body, he caught the edge of a wing tip through the starboard side of the cockpit over the right wing. The other two aircraft seemed to be flying off at tangents to this one.

As if she anticipated his question, Emma Shaw told him, as the Interceptor started leveling out, "We're so fast, Doctor, that my wingmen will take up positions better than a mile off in each direction. That way, a sensor fix won't catch all of us, and whoever might get caught has a better chance of evading a hit, a lot more maneuvering room, and the possibility that one or both of the other two aircraft can disable an incoming. But, relax," she said, the Interceptor finally in level flight. "We can outrun any missile they've got, at least as far as we know. And we can maneuver right alongside one."

"Let's not do that unless we can't avoid it, okay?" Rourke smiled.

166

Emma Shaw laughed. Her laugh wasn't one of those meaningless titters some women made no matter what was said, but a genuine laugh. "I'm not implying we're invincible, but if we can avoid getting picked up by two missiles at once, we've got a real chance of evading a hit. And, with any luck, we'll get in and out without getting spotted. At least, so far so good."

Terrain following, they were at relatively low speed, but he estimated they should be spotting Annie, Paul, Natalia, and the others in under sixty seconds, unless something had gone radically wrong. . . .

Annie Rubenstein looked up.

"Ohh, God," she whispered. There was a black shape coming in fast from the north. It was an aircraft but looked like none she had ever seen before. It was the shape of a fighter plane but considerably larger, its wings—although it was hard to tell from her perspective—almost appearing to be swept forward. "Paul! Natalia! Overhead!"

She choked up on the reins of the two horses she led, following the aircraft with her eyes as it streaked overhead. In the distance, she thought she heard the sounds of other aircraft. If these were enemy planes, they were done for.

As her eyes followed the aircraft—it was banking to starboard now, almost unbelievably rapidly—she saw the faces of the women who rode the horses she led.

There was terror in their eyes. . . .

Natalia ran beside Martin Zimmer, urging him to move faster by prodding his rib cage with the muzzle of her assault rifle. "Now. Get down here!" She half shoved

167

him into the snowbank, throwing herself down beside him, bringing the butt of the assault rifle to her shoulder. "Try anything and I will kill you," she told him.

But Martin Zimmer only laughed. The aircraft was touching down on the snowfield in the V-stol mode.

Paul Rubenstein dropped down beside his wife, telling her, "Now you stay here." He didn't bother telling her when to shoot or not to shoot. She was as good at this sort of thing as he was, possibly better. He kept to a crouch as he ran along the ridge of rock and snow, his eyes on the aircraft.

The plane was unmarked, a dull matte black.

Steam blew off its engine cowlings.

A door opened on the portside of the fuselage.

Paul Rubenstein threw himself flat into the snow, the Schmiesser up to his shoulder. Range was satisfactory to use it, and he was more confident with this weapon than with any of the new long arms they were given.

A man stepped out of the doorway.

"Hi, honeys, I'm home!" The voice was that of John Rourke. Paul Rubenstein started to laugh.

Chapter Thirty

It was the first time John Rourke had seen this coast-line from the air in any real detail, and it shocked him.

On The Night. Of The War, the major fault lines in California slipped and there was earthquake activity beyond measurement, much of California falling away. Mountain passes became fjords like those in Norway, low-lying desert became ocean, millions of people died.

Port Reno, Nevada was at the butt end of a long fjord, which was among the busiest shipping areas in the world, the fjord and the harbor into which it led a natural protection against storms. It was also the perfect place for submarines.

The newest vessels of the United States fleet were a magnificent sight to behold. They were enormous by any previously considered standard, but size aside, their versatility was what amazed John Rourke the most. The vessels combined the attributes of submarine and aircraft carrier at once, and they were capable of surface or submerged operation with equal grace.

They were the concept of the fighting seagoing ship taken to an inevitable conclusion, which began centuries before the birth of Christ. "What a Viking or a Phoenician would have done with one of these," John Rourke remarked to Emma Shaw.

"Like they say, 'You ain't seen nothin' yet,' Doctor." She took down a small microphone that nested in an overhead console. "This is Commander Shaw. All personnel please check seat restraints. We will be accomplishing air-sea transition in approximately two minutes."

"Transition," Rourke repeated. "As a physician six centuries ago, when I used the word *transition,* it usually meant that the termination of pregnancy was imminent and the expectant mother, if her husband was within earshot, occasionally became rather nasty."

Emma Shaw laughed. "We're airborne now, of course, and we could land on the deck of one of the vessels that is surfaced, but our orders are to land on one that isn't."

"We're going to land on a submerged runway?"

"We're going to land in a submerged dock, Doc," she grinned.

"How?" John Rourke asked.

"Interceptors are versatile, as I told you. We can shift from air mobile to sea mobile, consequently the aircraft becomes a mini-sub of sorts. But Interceptors aren't designed to be used as submarines, of course. What the dual capabilities mean is that we can travel underwater and dock underwater. Look at it in the context of a naval battle. We've got enemy ships all around us, right? What'll we do to launch aircraft to attack those surface ships and save everybody's bacon?"

Before John Rourke could hazard a guess, Emma answered her own question. "Easy. We launch our planes while submerged. The planes travel out of the battle zone while in the underwater mode, then accomplish a sea-air transition into the air. Now, a missile can knock out a conventional aircraft trying to get away from a conventional aircraft carrier, because the aircraft is so much involved in takeoff procedures and it's traveling relatively slowly along a fixed path. We're out the door and gone before they know it, and when we come out of the water,

170

we can be at Mach II in under sixty seconds."

She checked a timer on her console, then announced through the hand microphone, "I know none of you have done this before, but trust me, we'll be fine. Sorry there aren't any portholes for you to look out, because even after all the times I've done this, I still feel like saying 'wow.' Remember, don't undo seat restraints until we are docked and I give the okay."

She renested the microphone. "I've never been pregnant so I don't know much about that other kind of transition, but I'll take your word for it, Doctor."

"So long as you know about this kind, I'll be perfectly happy," Rourke said honestly.

The water was coming up fast and it didn't look as though the Interceptor was slowing at all. . . .

Marie Hayes was a pretty girl, her softly arranged hair, parted at the middle, so brown it was almost black. Her skin was flawless and fair, her eyes as dark a brown as her hair. She looked almost fragile, and despite the helmet that covered her hair now and the mannish-looking flight suit and bomber jacket she wore, she seemed terribly feminine.

Natalia Tiemerovna occupied the copilot's seat beside Marie Hayes. But her eyes weren't on Marie Hayes at all. After the first few minutes of being airborne, Natalia decided that she and the eight freed captives were in perfectly safe hands.

She reminded herself of that now as Marie Hayes murmured to her, "We're accomplishing air-sea transition, Major. Don't be alarmed. When I told our passengers there was nothing to it, I meant it. But it is kind of fun."

Natalia reserved judgment on that. The aircraft piloted

171

by Commander Shaw seemed to skate over the water, then disappear in a great white foamy wake.

Natalia braced herself as Marie Hayes leveled off, then dipped the Interceptor's nose slightly. "Hittin' the salt deck, Major. The fun starts now."

There was a thud, like a rough touchdown in a commercial aircraft, and suddenly a wake of ocean water surrounded them to port and starboard. The Interceptor's nose cut through into the apex of the wedge and downward, water rolling over the canopy surrounding them.

Marie Hayes's hands were virtually flying over the controls as Natalia glanced toward the woman for reassurance.

The ocean surrounded them, but they were still moving, almost as fast, it seemed, as before, broad arcs of landing lights illuminating the water ahead, schools of fish scurrying from their path.

The Interceptor banked, just as it would in the air, course correcting.

And ahead of them, there was an incredibly bright light.

The light grew brighter and brighter. And there was a shape behind the light, hulking, enormous.

Then they were past the light, the Interceptor slowing almost imperceptibly at first.

The shape took greater definition now. More lights spread ahead of them.

The shape was an enormous flooded docking bay, what little she could see of the color rust-brown except for the runway surface.

And now the Interceptor slowed dramatically, then stopped, moving forward only slightly in the current it had generated, touching down on the runway surface.

Marie Hayes snatched her microphone from the over-

172

head nest. "We've touched down and everything is fine. We have one more Interceptor to bring in, then the compartment will be pressurized. That'll take a few minutes. For safety's sake, please keep belted in." Then she turned toward Natalia. "See? A snap. But it's neat." She put her helmet microphone to her lips and spoke into it.

But Natalia was too fascinated to listen to standard touchdown talk.

She stared.

The docking bay was enormous. Well off in the distance, farther inboard, through the still-swirling waters, she could see more aircraft, as if waiting there.

She could not tell that aircraft belonged to Commander Shaw.

"Look around over there to your right and you'll see Wally Theodore coming in," Marie Hayes enthused.

Natalia Tiemerovna had always thought that once all sense of wonder was gone, it would be time to lay down and die. She felt that sense of wonder now. She could see the aircraft coming through the water toward them at what looked like enormous speed, landing lights brightly illumined, the water seeming to part around it because of the speed at which it traveled.

Logically, she knew that speed couldn't be too great, because the resistance of the water would have torn off the wings.

But still, she thought.

And then the Interceptor stopped, darker against the grey blackness, hovering there, then touching down as gently as a bird might come to rest on a branch.

And it was on the deck.

Klaxons sounded, audible through the water.

There was a terribly loud groaning sound, and for

173

a moment, Natalia thought something was wrong.

But she was still looking toward the entrance to the bay. And in the diffused light she could see doors, enormous like everything else here, starting to close, but not in any conventional manner.

Each door was like the iris of a camera, a series of comparatively small panels, fanning outward and sealing away the ocean itself. "Might want to swallow a little. Sometimes they pressurize a little too fast." Marie Hayes repeated the admonition through her microphone, to the passengers aft.

Jets of compressed air blew against the water, lowering the level just above the cockpit canopy now, then rolling away on both sides.

Natalia swallowed hard to equalize the mounting air pressure, as Marie Hayes activated toggle switches on an overhead panel and tiny jets of air blew into the cockpit.

The waters around them receded now.

Natalia could make out the first aircraft, the one Commander Shaw flew.

Marie Hayes started out of her seat, saying, "We're okay now, Major."

"Natalia, please," Natalia insisted.

"Natalia, then," Marie smiled, shaking her hair free of her helmet.

Natalia unbuckled and followed Marie Hayes aft. None of the women rescued from the Land Pirates had ever flown before, as far as Natalia could determine. This must have been beyond belief.

"Okay, ladies. We'll be able to open up in another couple of seconds. Now, the deck can be a little slippery, and boy does it hurt when you fall on it," Marie laughed. "So be careful stepping out."

Natalia followed Marie to the door. Marie worked a

manual control panel, verifying from a computer screen readout that the water level was below the aircraft's fuselage.

Then Marie punched a button and the fuselage door began to unlock, folding inward and aft.

Marie stepped aside and Natalia stood in the doorway.

This was how she had imagined the future when she was a little girl. Technology, vast and wonderful.

The docking bay was a hangar of huge proportions, an overhead vaulted and sprawling above, steel glistening and wet.

There was a pneumatic hiss and steps began folding out of the fuselage. Natalia took them, stopped on the last tread, and stared.

Air currents still blew across the deck, drying the larger puddles away, excess water channeled into gutters fore and aft.

Natalia stepped onto the deck.

She looked toward the Interceptor flown by the third pilot, Wally Theodore. Annie was stepping down from it onto the deck. Behind her was Martin Zimmer, with Paul close behind him, gun drawn.

Natalia looked toward the first aircraft.

John stood in the doorway. She knew him well. He was amazed, as was she.

John started down the steps, setting foot on the deck.

Natalia waved. John waved back. She looked up at Marie Hayes, then, asking her, "Do you think I'd be able to get permission to learn to fly one of these?"

"I don't see why not, Major."

That thought was delicious.

Natalia savored it.

In a few moments, there would be time enough to worry over everything else. Michael was safe, she knew.

Soon they would be together. Evidently, Eden's war plans were being accelerated. There were still the problems attendant upon trading Martin Zimmer to Deitrich Zimmer in return for Deitrich's surgical skills being used to save Sarah.

But, for now, wonderment was enough.

Chapter Thirty-One

John Thomas Rourke submitted to a physical examination—but merely a cursory one—in order to satisfy the
captain of this vessel, his host, that a little cold weather
and some time in the Wildlands was not potentially fatal.
But it was done more to convince twenty-two of the
women that letting a real doctor examine them was not
tantamount to ritual suicide. Mary Ann numbly did what
she thought was expected of her, and the twenty-fourth
woman, injured during the crash of the helicopter, was
either equally as compliant or fatalistic enough to realize
she had no real choice.

The exam over, Rourke found a shower and stood under
it for a very long time, washing his hair and body several
times before he really felt clean. Fresh clothes from his
pack, his face clean shaven, he felt like a new man.

He, Annie, Paul, and Natalia were scheduled for a flight
to Hawaii, leaving within the hour, but there was a briefing scheduled before that in Captain Rahn's office.

John Rourke arrived before any other members of The
Family and was immediately ushered into Rahn's office.
Rahn stood at attention behind his desk, beginning the
conversation with, "General Rourke, I must apologize for
not being available to welcome you personally. . . ." He
came around the desk and offered his hand.

Rourke took it, interrupting and saying, "Captain, I'm
not really much used to being called a general, simply be-

cause I never considered myself to be one. And any and all apologies are accepted. I knew your ancestor, Admiral Rahn. He was a fine and intelligent man. I was very pleased to learn that his family has carried on such a splendid tradition of service to the country."

"Thank you, sir. Would you care for a seat?"

Rourke nodded and sat down.

Captain Rahn sat down as well. He started to speak, but there was a quick rap on the door and the secretary, a pretty enough young woman, opened the door and announced, "Major Tiemerovna and Mr. and Mrs. Rubenstein, sir."

Rourke stood for the two women, waited until handshakes and pleasantries were exchanged and the women were seated, then sat down again.

Captain Rahn stood and walked across the room toward a good-sized video screen, mounted on an interior bulkhead. He glanced at a diver's watch on his left wrist and seemed to compare it to a military time diode counter beneath the screen. "There is a video transmission from Fleet Admiral Hayes, just about now." The screen came alive and there was static. "We're still working on scrambling high security satellite video, and sometimes it's like this. My apologies."

The picture cleared, not perfectly, but rather like UHF antenna reception on a sunny day. It was perfectly visible, if rather imperfect in resolution. The woman on the screen — somewhere in her middle fifties, as Rourke judged her — was attractive, and the resemblance between Admiral Hayes and her niece, whom Rourke had met briefly in the landing bay, was pronounced.

"Dr. Rourke. this is a true privilege, sir."

Rourke assumed the video screen somehow had a built-in camera and that just like something out of a science fiction movie, they could carry on a conversation as if they were in the same room. "The pleasure is mine, Admiral. May I introduce my family. To my right is my daughter, Annie, Mrs. Rubenstein. Beside her, her husband and my friend, Paul Rubenstein. The lovely woman to my right is Major Natalia Tiemerovna."

"This is like strolling through the pages of a history book," Admiral Hayes said, smiling. John Rourke was beginning to feel like a cross between Methuselah and one of the mammoths in General Verakov's office without walls in the Chicago's Field Museum of Natural History. Admiral Hayes went on, saying, "I'm looking forward to meeting with all of you personally at Pearl Harbor. I'm at Mid-Wake for the moment but should arrive in Hawaii shortly after all of you do. I have a lovely house overlooking the ocean. I was born in Mid-Wake, and I have a fondness for the ocean. I'd love all of you to come and share the view with me and dinner as well, at your earliest convenience."

"I'm certain, Admiral," Rourke said, "that I speak for my entire family, my son Michael as well, when I say that it would be our privilege and we eagerly await your invitation."

She smiled.

Rourke smiled.

"What are your plans concerning Martin Zimmer?" she asked at last.

"He goes with us," Rourke answered flatly.

"He is the head of state of Eden, Doctor. Are you sure—"

"The man who raised him, Admiral Hayes, unless I am mistaken is the only man in the world who has a prayer of saving the life of my wife. When I first was awakened from cryogenic sleep after emerging from my coma, I made it my business to research as quickly as possible what progress medical science had made in the years while I slept. Indeed, that progress was astonishing. However, to the

179

best I was able to ascertain, medical science had not per-
fected the skills necessary—surgical procedures, shall we
say—that would enable my wife to be brought back among
the living.

"Yet, Dr. Deitrich Zimmer possessed these skills more
than a century ago. He still does. As long as I have Martin Zimmer, I can force Deitrich Zimmer to save the life of
my wife. Without Martin, my wife is doomed to cryogenic
sleep . . . perhaps for years, perhaps for decades, perhaps
forever. I have no choice."

"What if, I were to order you to release him?" Admiral
Hayes asked, her smile faded.

"Order away, madam, no offense intended. He'll be released prematurely over my dead body."

"Mine as well," Natalia added.

"Ours," Paul said.

Admiral Hayes's smile returned. "I understand, through
a similar conversation with your son—who has just landed
at Pearl, by the way—that Martin Zimmer is also your
son?"

"My wife was shot in the head by Deitrich Zimmer only
a few moments after bearing our third child. That child
was a boy. Deitrich Zimmer kidnapped the infant son—
only a few hours older—of Lieutenant Martha Larrimore,
one of the Eden survivors. It was assumed Lieutenant Larrimore's child died in the clinic fire and explosions. That
was not the case. When Deitrich Zimmer murdered a
baby before the eyes of my children, my son-in-law, and
Major Tiemerovna, it was erroneously assumed that the
baby was the child to whom my wife gave birth. DNA typ-
ing and other similar tests were not available.

"In reality, the son of Martha Larrimore was murdered
instead," Rourke went on. "Zimmer raised Sarah's and my
son as his own, inculcating Nazism in the lad, but also
tampering with his genetic structure somehow. My knowl-

180

edge of genetic micro-surgery is a bit remiss, I'm afraid, but I intend to add to it at my first opportunity.

"However, you may rest assured I have no intention of murdering Martin Zimmer," Admiral Hayes's eyes narrowed as Rourke added a cautionary "—for the moment. If I am able to make a deal with Deitrich Zimmer, I will keep my part of the bargain. Martin will be returned. But since I helped to bring Martin Zimmer into the world, I feel it incumbent upon me to help rid the world of his evil. My eventual intentions are not at issue currently. I hope I have fully answered your question."

Admiral Hayes did not smile. "For the record, Doctor, should we attempt to have Martin Zimmer returned to Eden, you would prevent it to the best of your ability?"

"I would endeavor to prevent it, Admiral, to an extent you might not be able to well imagine. This I swear."

Admiral Hayes smiled enigmatically, then merely said, "Until later then, sir."

Chapter Thirty-Two

Hawaii. Palm trees on the white sand beaches, unspoiled highlands rich in vegetation, snow-capped mountains and a live volcano building more of the islands every moment.

He had never before visited there.

His father had evidently been a fan of Tom Selleck and, at The Retreat, had several episodes of the actor's long-running television series recorded, along with numerous of his films. The television series was set in Hawaii. Until now, that was the only image of Hawaii Michael Rourke had had.

The palms still swayed, but the breezes were apparently not quite so balmy. Aloha shirts were in evidence—there were civilian employees at Pearl Harbor—but this traditional attire was augmented by a windbreaker over it or a turtleneck under it.

In one case, Michael Rourke actually saw an aloha-patterned sweater.

He had wanted to walk, to stretch his legs after the long and boring flight from New Caracas to Honolulu. A technique was used, apparently commonplace now, that he remembered as a young boy reading about in a science magazine. The aircraft on which he had traveled merely climbed into the upper atmosphere, then reinserted, reducing flight time dramatically.

But it was still too long. He wanted to be active, to move about, to work the kinks out of his wounded legs.

Although he experienced a little pain as he moved, the stiffness was worse.

When he'd requested some time from the navy brass who'd met him, just to walk about the base and familiarize himself with the place, he'd also asked, "Will I start a small riot carrying a gun?"

Several of the navy personnel laughed. One of them, a lieutenant commander in Intelligence, told him, "Mr. Rourke, Mid-Wake encouraged an armed tradition as a means of staying alive. Since moving to the surface, that tradition has been reinforced. Now, in the city, weapons are usually carried concealed, except for an assault rifle or a shotgun in the window of a truck or van. But on the base, everyone's armed. You can't get onto the base without a security pass, military or civilian. So feel free."

And he bestowed on Michael a plastic-laminated identity badge labeled "V.I.P. Visitor," then printing out Michael's name as well.

"We'll have a permanent badge for you within the hour, just as soon as you smile for the ensign here so your picture can be taken."

Michael smiled at the pretty ensign. She was in her mid-twenties, a redhead and cute.

She took his picture with something the size of a cigarette pack, then told him, "Thank you, sir."

Perhaps to keep him from getting lost, perhaps just to keep him, the young ensign was assigned to accompany Michael.

Pearl Harbor, along with all other structures on the islands, was swept clean by the fires of The Great Conflagration, so nothing remained except, curiously, some minor bits of wreckage from the battleship *Arizona,* sunk during the original attack by the Japanese on December 7, 1941.

A new monument to it had been built, this one of the

first spots on the tour the young ensign—her name was Harriet Collins—was apparently giving him, whether he wanted a tour or not. But he was enjoying it. Aside from vaguely remembered trips as a boy Before The Night Of The War, he had never been a tourist.

Marine and naval personnel were everywhere, and security at the facility seemed tight. No one was without an identity badge, and as the lieutenant commander had told him, everyone was armed.

They left the memorial, taking a launch to the far side of the base where the airfield was situated. The airfield stretched farther than he could see, hangars flanking it on two sides, several control towers, various radar and other sensing installations in evidence. There were six principal runways, she told him, and during scramble drills it was possible to launch an aircraft every thirty-nine seconds.

Pearl Harbor seemed ready, but Michael wondered if it were ready enough.

Croenberg's plans to use sabotage to knock out power facilities, communications, and cause general disruption, coupled with an electromagnetic pulse over the fleet, might make all these preparations useless. Air defenses would be blinded, the aircraft on the ground and in the air within reach of the pulse would be dead until major repairs from shielded parts could be accomplished, and it would be down to guns, knives, and knuckles to defend these islands.

And the free world.

As before in history, the United States was the linchpin of an alliance against a terrible aggressor. Should the United States—Hawaii and Mid-Wake in this century—fail, the alliance would certainly crumble.

Which was, of course, what Martin and Deitrich Zimmer and Croenberg and all the others counted on.

Chapter Thirty-Three

John Thomas Rourke sat in the copilot's seat of the Interceptor, reading from a video screen that was set into a folding console. What he was reading was the Intell digest concerning his son Michael's report on the forthcoming attack on Pearl Harbor.

Michael had not only acted bravely but also well. Both of his children had grown to be people of whom he was terribly and justifiably proud.

Over the ages, various philosophers had held a cyclical view of history; and history, it seemed, was bearing out their contentions.

But it was also apparent that missed opportunities were gone forever, somehow escaping the cycle of repetition. If, following Germany's surrender at the close of World War II, those who had championed the idea of destroying world Communism had been heeded, the hostilities between the United States and Communist nations could have been avoided, together with suffering on both sides.

John Rourke recalled a conversation he had once had with a particularly bright and perceptive fifteen-year-old, a young man. In that fellow's case, the appellation "boy" would have been grossly inappropriate. Discussing the geopolitical situation at the time, Rourke had the usual adult prejudice: Listen to the young person, certainly; but learning from him would be highly improbable.

The young man had voiced an opinion that was at once

ruthless and practical: What was the sense in fighting a bitter and protracted war, conquering an enemy nation, then financing the rebuilding of said nation's economy, when it might potentially become an enemy power once again?

Certainly help in the rebuilding, but toward a better purpose.

Further exploring this idea with the young man, there was no evidence of malice in the fellow's thinking. Punishing a former enemy was not only inhumane but also counterproductive. Why not simply bring that nation into the fold, as it were?

A bit simplistic, yes, Rourke thought at the time, but when considered in the light of the form of government of the United States, as opposed to less free states, the idea of imposing such a comparatively enlightened form of government on a conquered nation that was annexed had considerable merit, most particularly to the conquered nation.

This was not a perfect solution, certainly, nor was it perfect when the Romans had, indeed, practiced it, imposing the Pax Romana on the then known world. But the Roman system was vastly less close to perfection than the American system.

Had the United States and her allies taken this additional step following World War II, none of what ensued would have happened.

John Rourke did not consider himself politically naive, and any solution viewed simplistically was dangerous. Divisiveness could have arisen between the allies, to be sure, and there might have been other unforeseen pitfalls. Yet, none of this could conceivably have been worse than what did happen.

But, perhaps, the United States of those days was too politically self-conscious, rather like the pretty girl at a party who doesn't realize she is pretty at all and, instead of dancing every dance, becomes a wallflower. Was it modesty or a lack of self-confidence?

The world was heading into a new epoch of mortal conflict, more rapidly perhaps than this ultramodern aircraft sped over the Pacific now.

Six hundred and twenty-five years ago, he had been unable to do anything, unable to prevent a war that nearly destroyed all of humanity and the very fabric of the planet.

This time, he would not fail.

It was a silent pledge John Rourke made . . . to himself, to his God.

Such a pledge, although often the most difficult to fulfill, was the hardest to break.

This war would not happen while any honorable means presented itself by which the conflict could be prevented and breath remained in his body to work toward that end.

Conciliation to tyranny was incomprehensible to him, as well as objectively futile.

So he would make peace by destroying those who would inflict war once again on humanity.

He looked away from the screen, and realized that Emma Shaw was watching him. "Something wrong?" John Rourke asked her.

"No. I was just looking at you. I'm sorry. It was rude of me, I guess."

Rourke didn't know what to say.

But, as he had learned, silence was nothing Emma Shaw allowed to last. "I'm a shameless hussy."

"What? I haven't heard that word in years!" Rourke exclaimed, smiling.

"Women are more direct these days, Doctor. I like you."

"Well, I like you, too," Rourke told her honestly.

"No, I mean I like you."

"I don't follow you," John Rourke responded.

Emma Shaw let her laugh happen again. "We're heading into a war, Doctor. One of these babies" — she patted the instrument console in front of her — "can outrun or outfight almost anything. But accidents happen. Life expectancy's

187

close to a hundred these days, in case you didn't know. But people still die, all the time. I learned a long time ago that life isn't something you can count on to be there, that the breath you have inside of you might be the last breath you'll ever experience. So, I figured it was best to be honest.

"When I was a little girl," she went on, "I used to say the damndest things. I know my parents must have wanted to dig a hole sometimes and crawl into it out of sheer embarrassment. I guess I haven't changed much, and I know saying this to a man like you is perfectly silly. But, if you're ever lonely, you don't have to be alone."

She looked away.

John Rourke said nothing. The idea was a little amusing—not what she'd just said; that was sweet. But the realization her words brought to him was what amused him.

Perhaps he should have consulted with that rather astute fifteen-year-old concerning advice about women, too.

By circumstance alone, the most confusing and morally troubling relationship of his entire life had been resolved. Natalia was Michael's now.

He'd never thought he wanted to be free of her, and he still loved her and always would.

But he was free, now, free to be Sarah's husband when she was revived, restored to him.

Emma Shaw was not only pretty—in a much earthier, less incredible way than Natalia—but she was also attractive to him as a person. He liked independent women. He'd never cared for a woman who shrunk from life, was afraid of challenge.

But, never again.

Chapter Thirty-Four

Michael Rourke stood on the runway as the fuselage door of the first of three unmarked Interceptors to land opened and his father stepped out.

John Rourke smiled, and as he moved down the steps almost in the same instant in which they folded out, he unslung a medium-sized black duffle bag, just carrying it in his hand.

He stopped about two feet from Michael, setting down the bag. "You did well, son."

John Rourke extended his right hand.

Michael Rourke clasped it.

Then John Rourke's smile broadened even more. "You're not too old; give me a hug, damnit." And they embraced, quickly, each stepping back from the other, Michael feeling a smile breaking out on his face. John Rourke nodded his head toward the black duffle, saying, "Got your handguns and your knife there. Figured you might need them. Nice Uzi carbine. Reproduction?"

"One of the Lancers."

"Yours or borrowed?"

"Germans gave it to me," Michael smiled again, shrugging.

"A very underappreciated firearm in its day, that semi-auto carbine. Have to let me try it sometime." John Rourke cleared his throat. "You did well with playing spy. Understand you took one getting away."

The wind blew hard and cool over the tarmac as Natalia climbed down out of one of the aircraft. Michael wanted to take her into his arms. "Like they say in the movies, 'Just knicked me.' I'm fine."

John Rourke glanced back over his shoulder. "So, what are you waiting for?"

Michael didn't understand.

"Natalia . . . son. But don't forget to give your sister a hug and say hi to Paul, huh?"

"Can you . . . uh . . ."

"I'll get the bag dropped off in your quarters. Go on."

Michael nodded, clapped his father on the shoulder, then broke into a hobbling run across the field toward Natalia. His right hand held the Uzi against his body so it wouldn't pendulum against him as he moved.

Natalia saw him and started walking, then running, into his arms. "Michael!" Her arms went around his neck and he crushed her against him, kissing her harder than he'd ever kissed her, then just holding her. . . .

John Thomas Rourke watched Michael and Natalia.

What they had seemed very good.

He picked up the duffle bag and started to walk toward the knot of naval brass about a hundred yards distant. . . .

Annie Rourke Rubenstein had left Martin Zimmer handcuffed to one of the structural supports in the cabin bulkhead. Unless he was a magician, he wasn't going anywhere.

She stood halfway down the egress steps, Paul already standing on the tarmac. Over her husband's right shoulder, she watched her father.

Her skirts caught in the cool breeze off the sea. Annie

190

lifted her clothing with her left hand as she walked down the remaining steps and stood beside Paul, felt him reach out and take her hand.

The wind had her hair, too, but she did nothing to fight it, merely leaning her head against her husband's shoulder. "I love you."

"I know."

"I feel so sorry for him."

"Your dad?"

"Uh-huh. He's so alone. I have you. Michael has Natalia. He doesn't have anybody."

She felt Paul exhale, felt his hand gently turn her arm behind her and his arm bind her to him. "Your mother's down but not out. He'll make things right. Then they'll have each other."

"I don't think so," she told him, her head still against his shoulder.

"Psychic flash?"

If anyone else had said it that way, Annie would have thought she was being made fun of. But Paul never did that. She told him, "No. Not even woman's intuition. Maybe just odds for and against. Even if he gets her back, somehow I don't think he'll keep her."

"Sarah'd never—"

"It's different with you and me," Annie almost whispered, a catch in her throat. "And for Michael and Natalia, too. It's not the same for them. They love each other, but I don't think they like each other. And I think Dad knows it and so did Mom."

"Sufficient unto each day is the evil thereof," Paul quoted.

Annie didn't say anything. She hoped Paul was right. She prayed he was right. . . .

* * *

Emma Shaw watched John Rourke. She stood in the doorway, her helmet off, the rubber band out of her hair, which was blowing in the wind.

She'd made a fool out of herself. Dr. Rourke had been very polite, but she knew it anyway.

Maybe they'd never see each other again.

She rubbed the fingers of her right hand against her palm.

John Rourke shook her hand. He told her, "It's been great flying with you."

She wanted to fly with John Rourke very badly, more than she'd ever wanted anything in her life.

He stopped before a group of officers, both Naval and Marine Corps.

Where were the brass bands and the red carpets?

He was a living legend, come back from near death to try to save the world one more time, mankind's reluctant, quiet champion. And Emma Shaw wondered if they appreciated that. Because of all the impressions her few hours with Dr. John Thomas Rourke engendered in her, the most indelible was that he was a quiet man who merely wanted to live his life.

Fate just refused to allow that.

Chapter Thirty-Five

Considering the propensity for size—the Intercepter fighter aircraft, the carrier-sized vessels that doubled as surface and submarine warfare vessels, even the acreage of the Pearl Harbor base itself—the conference room was rather small, even appearing crowded.

Video screens dominated three of the four walls, showing maps, intelligence overflight photos, and the like.

A podium, apparently equipped with sophisticated electronics that enabled the speaker to utilize any or all of the screens individually or simultaneously, dominated the fourth wall, into which were set the pneumatic double sliding doors through that the room was accessed.

There were more names and faces than he could, at this point in time, differentiate. And the name tags on each person's respective uniform obviated the necessity for memorization.

John Rourke listened instead of talking.

The current speaker was a marine colonel, introduced as being in charge of physical security for the Island of Oahu in general and Pearl Harbor specifically.

He was generously built, broad-shouldered and tall, with a haircut short in comparison to those of his fellow officers that he looked as though he'd slipped through a time warp from the sixties. But, in sharp contrast to his appearance, his voice was a gentle, warm-sounding, mellifluous baritone as he said, "Depending on their choice of weaponry, we could experience unacceptably severe casualty levels. Eden's gas capabilities have been talked about, there've been tantalizing hints, but nothing definite. If they use chemical agents, we just flat out don't have enough protective gear available. And, unless they hold off on attacking for the next six months, we would never have enough equipment to protect the civilian population.

"The question, it seems, is how can we interdict enemy action, rather than respond to it. I'll open the floor to any comments or what-have-you before I go on here. . . ."

"Colonel?"

The man looked up from his notes. "General Rourke, yes, sir?"

John Rourke had almost given up on encouraging people to stop calling him general, so he ignored it. "You spoke before about computer models."

"Yes, sir."

"Wouldn't the Eden Defense Forces' strategic planners have access to your computer modeling programs . . . I mean, in their generic form?

"I . . . uh . . . I hadn't thought of that, sir. I—"

"My point, Colonel," Rourke went on, "is that if we stay with computer models, can't the enemy obviate any effectiveness such counterplanning might have by simply running the same basic programs, only more completely? I mean, we'll be guessing at many of the details, of course, unless your medical personnel can get information out of our guest, Martin Zimmer. But from the briefing my son went through, it wouldn't seem the sit-reps Croenberg and the other SS personnel are running are that detailed.

"So," Rourke continued, "we should probably assume they'll have a better grasp of their plans than we will. Which means their computer models can be more complete. They should be able to anticipate and plan for countering every move we'd make."

"I . . . uh . . . I never thought of that, sir. We use computer models . . ."

John Rourke ignored the fact that no one in the room smoked, took one of the German non-carcinogenic cigarettes from his shirt pocket, and lit it in the blue yellow flame of his battered Zippo. A cigar would have been socially objectionable. "When I was in the intelligence profession, several years Before The Night Of The War, of course, we had a similar problem." Rourke exhaled smoke. Several of the personnel in the room looked shocked. A few looked amused. One lit up as well.

Then Natalia lit a cigarette and so did Michael. John Rourke made a mental note to talk with his son about smoking. But for now he went on, saying, "I knew a very fine gentleman who wound up in the intelligence profession—or perhaps counterintelligence is more apt—when he was little more than a boy. He stuck with it in one manner or another throughout his entire life. He once remarked to me that the problem in strategic planning was that none of the planners were doers. That was possibly a bit harsh a criticism, but the fact remains that he was making an interesting point.

"Consider this," Rourke continued. "If you and your enemies use similar or perhaps even identical programs, you're planning around each other. And everything is conventional, because all the responses are from the computer, and that means everything it will come up with has been thought of and used or discarded before. You're limiting your options. Why?"

"Why, sir?"

"Why?"

"Well . . . uh . . ."

"I can take it, Colonel. Why?"

195

The colonel looked as though he felt a bit awkward. Rourke knew he was being nasty, but he had to make his point.

After a pause of several seconds, the colonel said, "That's . . . uh . . . that's the way it is done, sir."

"Has anyone in this room—aside from members of my family, of course—ever killed anyone? Let's see hands." No one raised a hand. "Has anyone ever met an enemy agent other than during a social function?" No hands. "Has anyone ever been part of a combat situation other than an exercise?" No hands.

John Rourke smiled but said nothing else.

The colonel did not speak for a moment. Then, "What are you suggesting, sir?"

John Rourke flicked ashes from his cigarette into the palm of his hand. One of the senior officers said something to one of the junior officers present as an aide, and the man practically sprinted from his seat, presumably for ashtrays. "I didn't mean to put you on the spot, Colonel. And this is really none of my business, I suppose. I was very impressed with your briefing. I mean that sincerely, but I thought that a point needed to be made. You wound up as the scapegoat. That point is, if we want to stop the saboteurs and the commando teams we're expecting here, the best way might be to outthink them rather than to try out-computing them, possibly in vain."

"Hear, hear!" The voice, a woman's, came from the rear of the room.

Someone to Rourke's right started to applaud. The applause spread.

John Rourke flicked more ashes into his left palm. . . .

This meeting was more to John Rourke's liking. The colonel in charge of security—his name was Roy Stoddard—was present, as was a naval psychiatric specialist, Helen Stickley, the commander of the SEAL team based out of Pearl, Lieutenant Commander Grant Washington, and Fleet Admiral Hayes, barely off her personal Interceptor from Mid-Wake.

Admiral Hayes was saying, "Dr. Rourke, like it or not, you're still on the payroll. Your salary had been accumulating and earning interest for one hundred and twenty-five years. You are a millionaire several times over. But my point, General, is that I do have the right to order you to stay physically uninvolved with these coming matters. You are, sir, a national treasure. . . ."

"Don't be ridiculous, Admiral. And what am I going to do with all that money?"

"The money is your problem. Build yourself another survival retreat if you want. But you are a national treasure. As such, I cannot allow you to risk your life. . . ."

"No disrespect meant, Admiral, but no one allows or disallows me to do anything of which I'm able. I can be of help here, and unless you attempt to force your will upon me, I intend to help."

Admiral Hayes shook her head. "If I get you killed . . ."

"If I die, it's my fault not yours. So, can we get back to the matter at hand?"

She nodded only, then looked at the psychiatrist. "Doctor, you have results?"

"Yes, Admiral. I personally supervised the administration of several rather powerful truth-inducing drugs to Martin Zimmer—after, of course, running him through a thorough physical examination. The transcript of text should come up on that screen." Helen Stickley gestured toward a large screen on the far wall of Admiral Hayes's office. John Rourke reflected that a television repairman could well have made a fortune these days, with the proliferation of video and computer screens for information dissemination. Martin Zimmers' face appeared on the screen in reasonably tight close-up, his words — occasionally unintelligible — scrolling away across the bottom of the screen beneath his face. "Part of the time — and that's usual under these circumstances — Mr. Zimmer's speech appears slurred and unintelligible."

"Can we fast-forward into the part you mentioned, Doctor?" Admiral Hayes asked, interrupting.

Dr. Stickley was a civilian, but evidently well used to the military. She touched a control on the arm of her chair, and the presentation started moving at what Rourke estimated was roughly three times normal speed. The scrolling was impossible to read and Martin Zimmer's face looked almost funny — but not quite.

When the tape returned to normal speed, Martin's speech was clear again. He was picked up in mid sentence, saying, ". . . along on the setup. A house on Sebastian's Reef . . ." Dr. Stickley paused the tape. "Sebastian's Reef, Dr. Rourke, is named after Commander Sebastian, later Admiral Sebastian."

"I knew the gentleman," John Rourke nodded.

"It's a rather exclusive civilian enclave on the far side of the island."

"Numerous estate-sized houses set within a natural enclave of woods," Admiral Hayes interjected. "I was going to recommend to you that you might consider that area, Dr. Rourke. You could afford it."

The tape continued, Martin saying, "The house is the headquarters for the SS sabotage units on Oahu, Croenberg said once."

Dr. Stickley's voice was on the tape now. "Only this man Croenberg mentioned it? Did you discuss this with anyone else in your organization? Answer the question, Martin."

"Nobody. Dad thinks . . ." The word shocked John

198

Rourke.

Dr. Stickley said, "He is referring to someone named Deitrich Zimmer, Dr. Rourke."

"I realized that," Rourke responded, his voice almost a whisper.

She wound the tape back a little. "Dad thinks that the fewer details any of us know, the less chance for a leak."

"Dad was right," Rourke observed.

"Apparently," the colonel said.

The tape was paused.

Lieutenant Commander Washington asked, "Admiral, may I make a suggestion?"

"Certainly, Mr. Washington."

"Ma'am, I think we could mount an operation against that house right now and not only interdict some of their plans, but perhaps get a line on future activities. Maybe throw a monkey wrench into their timetable a little."

John Rourke said, "This isn't a classic military operation, Admiral. If we hit in military fashion, we'll get them, but they'll have the opportunity to burn or degauss every record they've got. We'll wind up with some people, some weapons, and very little information. If what Martin Zimmer is saying is true, then most likely little of the information that might be stored there is in the heads of whoever we might net."

"What are you suggesting?" The colonel asked the question, and John Rourke turned and looked at him.

"Very simple, Colonel. Before The Night Of The War, in addition to teaching and writing concerning survivalism, as you may know, I also taught special weapons and tactics, usually to counterterrorist units, occasionally to police special response teams, SWAT teams, etc. What I propose is that Mr. Washington's SEAL team people, in conjunction with some of your security cops, be mobilized into the sort of operation we used to run when those

199

teams were hitting a terrorist safe house or on a big drug bust.

"If we just go in there and attack," Rourke went on, "we'll miss much of the value the raid could provide."

"My people are ready, Admiral," Washington volunteered.

Admiral Hayes stared at John Rourke. He stared back and she smiled. "So you've made yourself the indispensable man, haven't you, Doctor?"

John Rourke only said, "Hopefully."

Chapter Thirty-Six

Sebastian's Reef itself was a horseshoe of black coral extending more than thirteen miles. Waves crested over it, breaking into almost infinite patterns of white froth whipped into the lagoon beyond on the driving wind.

John Thomas Rourke sat in the helicopter's copilot's seat, Emma Shaw at the machine's controls. He had been told by Admiral Hayes that a personal pilot would be available to him. When he learned the designated pilot was Emma Shaw, he'd evidently looked surprised. Asked if there was something unsuitable about Commander Shaw, Rourke had replied not at all.

And she wasn't what he'd come to expect as her usual rather loquacious self. In khaki shirt and slacks and a blue baseball cap with her unit designation on the front, she merely sat there, staring ahead, her only words into her radio headset's mouthpiece, or to ask if she was passing low enough or slowly enough, or if he required an additional flyby.

They'd come along the coast of Oahu, flying so close to the lapping surf that, at times, Rourke could almost feel the spray when he peered out through the open bubble.

They began following the reef as it first appeared, letting its course draw them inland.

And now they were over the sand, crossing it quickly as they climbed, then over the high rocks beyond, these grey and black, and volcanic, some in massive slabs, flat as a billiard table, others upthrusting and jagged, like the teeth of an enormous flesh-eating beast.

The trees started then, so densely planted as to form a canopy, almost impenetrable. Rourke was just about to comment on this, when Emma Shaw's voice came through his headset. "Once we're over this crest, Doctor, the ground drops off and the palm trees start."

"Thank you," Rourke responded.

In another second, the aircraft still climbing, the canopy began to break, Rourke noticing a wide path leading through the trees, from the palm tree-fronted house beyond toward the sea.

He consulted his map on the computer/video console folded out in front of him. Rourke pressed a button and superimposed the map image over the ground image below, the altitude compensator already adjusting image size. The name of the owners of the house, data concerning its size, etc. all appeared beneath the image.

Automatically, the program moved on as they left the house behind them. He'd asked before whether or not a helicopter flyby would alarm the personnel at the suspect house. He was told that helicopter traffic here was common, and as long as they did not seem to pay particular attention to one piece of property over another, there would be nothing to arouse interest.

The next house was larger than the first, mansion-sized, a small helipad in the front yard, a chopper only marginally smaller than the military aircraft in which they flew tethered there. Several private automobiles were in a parking area near a large garage beyond.

And then they were past this house. Emma Shaw's voice came again, saying, "I think that's the house, Doctor."

Indeed it was.

The house itself was much larger than the previous

structures, in the shape of a squared-off letter C. A fountain of considerable proportions was set in a graveled driveway, which ran through a wide grassy area, dotted with palm trees.

The house had two full stories and a third floor along the center, between the two legs of the C. Toward the north of the main structure was what appeared to be a guest house, a sprawling single-story, that was otherwise an architectural match to the main house. The driveway branched off between the main house and the guest house, leading to a garage that appeared designed to hold at least a dozen cars, a swimming pool, tennis courts, a building that his computer's video map indicated was a stable, and a wooded area.

The entire compound was fenced in.

Although he could have read the same thing from the screen, he remembered the colonel telling him, "The house was once the home of the Trans-Global Alliance, before that was moved to Switzerland about thirty-five years ago. It was built with enough meeting rooms, bedrooms, kitchens and recreational facilities to handle well over three dozen personnel, not to mention a staff which sometimes exceeded fifty people. Most of the staff lived in the guest house structure, except for those who might be required during the night—chief of security, night butler, night cook, and the like. Then, when the Alliance moved its headquarters, the place was bought by a German corporation. We never thought twice about it."

The helicopter arced away from the property, Emma Shaw apologizing, "If we make too much out—"

"I know," Rourke said, cutting her off.

He'd seen enough. . . .

"A fortress that doesn't look like one," John Rourke said

quietly, spreading his hands over the horizontal screen that filled the center of the planning table in the security bunker.

Michael, Natalia, Annie, and Paul were here, and he felt better, somehow.

The marine colonel whose security personnel John Rourke intended to utilize asked, "What are you planning, sir?"

"It goes back to what we were saying earlier, Colonel. Computer-generated scenarios can be anticipated. So can military operations, because basic military operational techniques are all but universal, aren't they? I imagine that someday, if mankind is that fortunate both to survive and be in the right place at the right time, should we encounter intelligent otherworldly beings, we'd likely discover that if the concept of a military is not unknown to them, the tactics would still be similar.

"What we want to do," Rourke went on, "is the unexpected. With your permission, Colonel, I'd like to plan this out in a totally different way. We'll require surveillance, penetration teams, and a lot of luck." John Rourke looked at the colonel, then at Lieutenant Commander Washington.

"Agreed, sir," the colonel said.

Chapter Thirty-Seven

The facade of the building, that happened to be on Rourke Boulevard (something John Rourke tried to ignore), was of a synthetic that looked and even felt like marble. The showroom floor and walls were of the same material, a highly polished black that looked positively elegant.

The showroom for Lancer Firearms reminded John Rourke of some of the elegant shops he'd seen on New York's Park Avenue when, away on business, he would hastily and guiltily shop for presents for Sarah and Michael and Annie.

But rather than overpriced baubles, the Lancer showroom was the most fully equipped weapons emporium he had ever seen, reminiscent of the great gunhouses like Abercrombie & Fitch or Chicago's Sundeen's, the staff knowledgeable, each item displayed impeccably presented.

"I am Walter Sutherland, sir. You may recognize the reproductions of many of your own firearms here, sir. Meeting you, I must say, Dr. Rourke, is an experience I shall treasure."

Walter Sutherland was a tall, very trim man, narrow shoulders accentuating his height, a receding hairline (baldness had been elective for the last century or so, Rourke understood, as it was now so easily prevented or corrected) heightening the thin, bony quality of his face. He wore a dark grey turtleneck and a black suit, the jacket without lapels in the once-again popular Nehru style.

All that was missing to give Walter Sutherland the image of the perfect aristocratic retail merchant were striped pants, a morning coat, and a white carnation in the lapel.

"Your facility is magnificent."

"I would love you—and your entire family—" Sutherland gestured toward Michael, Natalia, Paul, and Annie. "I would consider it a great honor should your schedules allow that you tour our manufacturing facilities just outside the city."

"I'd really enjoy that," John Rourke said sincerely. "And I'll surprise you one day and turn up on your doorstep. You have no idea how pleasant it is for a man from my era to find something like this."

Although everything was a reproduction, of course, there were fine English doubles—double rifles, rimfire-free pistols, single-actions in all the standard and the more exotic barrel lengths, even muzzle-loading flintlock and percussion rifles and pistols. Of edged weapons, there were designs Rourke remembered, as with the guns like long-ago friends once thought lost forever. Reproductions again, the touch of Crain, Crawford, Randall, and the other great knife makers of the Twentieth Century was everywhere in evidence.

Mr. Sutherland was saying, "With our edged weapons as with our firearms, sir, we strive to duplicate not only the design but the materials, every nuance of construction. In some cases, we have only scanty written records to go on, the occasional photograph, but at other times we have the original weapon to measure, to test, to reproduce. We do our humble best."

John Rourke stared into a case of Detonics .45s. He looked up from the case and into Sutherland's face. "Your 'humble best,' Mr. Sutherland, is peerless."

"Would you care to examine—"

John Rourke only smiled. He now understood the meaning of the old expression "happy as a kid in a candy store." "Of course," he almost whispered.

While Mr. Sutherland and John talked guns, Natalia merely inspected the cases. They had come here not for recreational purposes, although indeed it was pleasant, but to pick up whatever additional firearms they might require for the upcoming operation. She was not terribly taken with the "modern" firearms, either the caseless cartridge weapons or the energy weapons.

Certainly, these had their applications, and her taste in weaponry had always been eclectic. But she was wedded to the "older" guns, those from her own epoch. She remembered a story John had told her once, concerning the near-legendary western gunfighter Wild Bill Hickok. Long into the cartridge era, Hickok clung to his cap and ball revolvers, usually 1851 Navy Colts.

At the time, she had failed to understand why a man of such consummate skill at arms would reject the new in favor of the old. But John had told her that story over six centuries ago.

In the case before which she now stopped was the weapon she'd sought, her favorite large capacity 9mm pistol. "May I show you something, Major?"

She looked up into the face of a man who seemed almost cut from the same mold as his superior in the company's hierarchy, Mr. Sutherland.

"Yes. The SIG-Sauer P-226, please."

"Certainly, madam." And he began to open the case.

* * *

John Rourke had finished his tour of the showroom.

Mr. Sutherland said, "I understand that you and your family have some requirements. The government has offered to pay us, of course, but I would consider it a personal privilege to provide what you might need—in exchange for a small favor."

John Rourke looked at him. "Yes?"

"I would like the opportunity—at your convenience, of course, and under your eye, as it were—to examine your Detonics Combat Masters. We have duplicated the various Colt semi-automatics and the Detonics Scoremaster and Servicemaster, and we've tried with the Combat Masters, but I've never quite felt we had the details properly in mind, with no actual firearm to work from."

John Rourke drew back the sides of his battered brown leather bomber jacket, exposing the twin stainless Detonics .45s in their double Alessi shoulder rig. "At your convenience, sir, after this matter at hand."

"Certainly. I understand. Now, what can I help you with?"

John Rourke began walking along the showroom floor again. He stopped before a wall display. "The twelve-inch barreled Remington 870 Witness Protection shotgun with the pistol grip."

"With the fold-down fore-end piece?"

"No, a bit too bulky, I'm afraid." Rourke walked on, stopping again. "And my Steyr-Mannlicher SSG is in storage in a safe house at Eden City. I'm afraid I'll be without it for a time."

"I wish we could help you, Doctor, but we—"

"Would you like to make one?"

"I'd—"

"After I've retrieved it, you can borrow it if you like."

Sutherland's eyes positively beamed. "But I fail to see what we could provide—"

Rourke nodded his head toward the wall display. "Is that H-K 91 an accurate duplicate internally?"

"To the last detail, sir. Two of the originals were discovered twenty years ago in an abandoned survival bunker in Montana. I'm afraid they were smuggled out of Eden," Sutherland confided. "I wish we had available one of the sniper versions of the G-3, but none has turned up—not yet at least."

"If the 91 requires trigger work, can you perform it?"

"Certainly, sir."

Rourke nodded.

"We have some fine scopes: Kahles, Schmidt & Bender—"

Rourke shook his head. "I'll prefer the iron sights with the proper ammunition." Then Rourke walked toward one of the several display cases given over to fighting knives. "This is a reproduction of the OSS sleeve knife H.G. Long of England, produced for the American firm Ek, isn't it?"

"Indeed it is, Doctor."

"Then, if I may, I'd like it. But I would be more than happy to pay for these items. I'm told that I have one hundred and twenty-five years of brigadier general's pay and allowances banked away for me at interest. And you can still borrow the guns."

"No, sir. I insist. Consider this our way of saying thank you to you, sir, for what you have done and what I suspect you are about to do."

"Try," Rourke corrected.

"There is one thing."

"Certainly," Rourke said, smiling.

"Your knives. I've read about them—the Crain knife

and the A.G. Russell knife. I would love to duplicate them."

"Consider them available whenever you like, again following our immediate business."

Sutherland extended his hand. Rourke shook it.

Chapter Thirty-Eight

It was marvelous how some images stuck in the mind.

All the while John Rourke paced the balcony area outside the security offices, he kept expecting to see the actor Jack Lord, or at least someone who looked like him. Because the raid on the former Trans-Global Alliance headquarters, now a private home at Sebastian's Reef, was taking place in a civilian area, the Honolulu police were being brought in to assist. Although Sebastian's Reef was on the far side of the island, it was administered by the city of Honolulu.

Rourke thought that a fine idea, but at the back of his mind, as he looked through the picture window dominating the entire balcony and onto the grounds where military and civilian personnel went their way, he kept expecting to hear a craggy voice from behind him telling a young assistant to book a just-busted felon. Rourke didn't share his observations with the marine colonel who was in charge of security or with anyone else at the moment, either.

Television programs from more than six centuries ago weren't frequent topics of conversation.

He heard the footfalls first, then the voice, but by that time John Rourke was already turning around. The man he saw was a vigorous-looking late fifties or early sixties. With a life expectancy these days of around one hundred years, being in one's fifties or sixties wasn't anywhere near old.

The man was about five-feet-nine or so, broad-shouldered, barrel-chested, and stocky. His face had the "map of Ireland" all over it. "You're Dr. Rourke! What a pleasure, sir!" The man extended his right hand and John Rourke took it. "I'm Inspector Shaw . . . Tim Shaw, Doctor. I command Honolulu's Tactical Squad."

"The pleasure's mine." The name struck a familiar chord. "Shaw. Any relation to a pilot, Commander Emma Shaw?"

Tim Shaw grinned, white teeth flashing, his florid cheeks a little more florid-looking for the moment. "My daughter. Not only a damned fine pilot, but a looker, too. Emma's my girl."

"You should be very proud of her, Inspector."

"Tim, please."

"John, then."

"John," Tim Shaw nodded. They released hands. "Are you gonna be in on this, John?"

"The meeting, definitely. The raid, too. It'll be good to have you and your people with us. I view this as a police-style operation rather than a classic military job."

"Then before we go inside," Tim Shaw began, "maybe you should fill me in a little. I was told there was a joint operation coming up—all on the sly 'cause it was top secret—and to get my rear end over here."

John Rourke plucked a cigar from the pocket of his shirt, then remembered his manners. "Cigar?"

"You bet," Tim Shaw nodded, grinning. Rourke gave Shaw one of the thin, dark tobacco cigars, then lit them both in the blue-yellow flame of his Zippo. "Good cigar," Tim Shaw said, exhaling.

"Here's the job as I see it, Tim," Rourke told this man for whom he felt an instant liking. "We have Martin

Zimmer, the leader of Eden, a prisoner here. . . ."

"Whoa!"

"Exactly," Rourke nodded, exhaling. The smoke ricocheted off the glass, dissipating into the ventilating system. "My son — and myself, for that matter — bear a remarkable resemblance to Martin Zimmer."

"Should I read somethin' into that, John?"

"It's a long story, but Martin Zimmer is also my son. I'll explain it when there's the time. Suffice it to say, my son Michael can pass for Martin. He got away with it in Eden City itself."

"And?"

"We're going to try for a repeat performance, only this time with backup. We're going to let it out that Martin is on the island and has escaped. The people we're after will try to pick him up . . . will already be on alert for him, possibly."

"Who are these people?"

"Saboteurs sent by Eden, some of them or all of them SS personnel; Martin's government works hand in fist with the Nazis. These guys'll be tough, well set with weapons, and not afraid to use them. We know where they're at . . . the old Trans-Global Alliance estate on Sebastian's Reef."

"That place is built like a fort."

"Exactly why we need an inside man . . . my son Michael. He's agreed to do it, perhaps a little too readily. But he's a game guy. The idea behind the raid is to nail these saboteurs before they can do their jobs. There's an attack planned on the island in general and Pearl Harbor in particular. We don't know when, but likely it'll be soon. So, we want whatever documents, computer disks, anything that'll be of intelligence value, just as much as we want the men themselves. I don't know if there's a drug problem these days; I'd assume there isn't. . . ."

Tim Shaw laughed bitterly. "It's called 'Starlight.' It's a fast and dirty synthetic hallucinogenic, highly addictive. Guess where it's made?"

"Eden," Rourke suggested.

"You got it."

"My point is," John Rourke went on, "I see this thing like a drug raid, all right? No good to get the guys if you don't get the stuff, too. Unless the law has changed a lot."

"I don't know how much it's changed or not, Doctor, but if we don't nail 'em with the shit on them, we don't have a case."

"Then you know exactly where I'm coming from," Rourke nodded. "I'm sorry to hear that drugs are still a problem . . . or a problem again, however you look at it. But we have to get in there, hopefully get some of these guys alive—another reason I'm looking for a police-style raid rather than a military assault. We'll have Lieutenant Commander Washington's SEALs. . . ."

"Grant's a good man. His guys and our guys train together sometimes."

"That'll be good," Rourke said. "Let's go in."

"Should I look surprised when you—"

"No," Rourke smiled.

214

Chapter Thirty-Nine

He could sleep later, he told himself. And just in case he did die, a good memory would be better than a good rest. Michael slipped between Natalia's thighs, her arms enfolding him. "I love you, Michael," she whispered.

His lips touched her throat, her head leaning back, her hair—it was such a dark brown that it was almost, in defiance to nature, a true black—longer now than it had been when she was a grown very mysterious woman, and he was a very confused little boy.

She was the most beautiful woman he had ever seen, counting living people, ones in videotaped movies, better than anyone.

And now, because of the way his father had manipulated the cryogenic chambers, even though she was born nearly two decades before him, he was a nominal two years older than she. He had understood, as he grew to manhood in The Retreat, his sister his only companion, the nature of his father's plan. This woman was for him, from the elemental, practical consideration that the human race, should no life survive outside The Retreat, would require perpetuation and healthy babies did not come from a confined genetic pool. Natalia was for him, as Paul was for Annie.

In Paul and Annie's case, there was genuine love—from the first time they saw each other as adults and before. Michael would watch his sister as she watched Paul. It was more than his father's planning. She loved Paul then, even before they had ever met as adults.

He, on the other hand, had rejected loving Natalia.

And then, suddenly, a wife, later a mistress, it happened. Instead of coming to Natalia as a boy who, by design, had grown into manhood, he came to her as a widower, a man who had been with two women, fathering a child — who died — by one.

He simply realized he loved her . . . had all the time.

And she loved him.

At first, he had wondered if he were a mere substitute for his father, John more rigidly moral than he, perhaps, but certainly committed to a wife.

And then, John Rourke was near death, gone from them for what could have been forever, and — not because John Rourke was no longer on the scene, but because of their commonly felt loss — he and Natalia were drawn to each other.

And it happened.

As her thighs closed tightly around him and her body moved beneath him, something else happened. "I love you," Michael Rourke told Natalia Tiemerovna as his body collapsed over hers.

It might be the last time he ever had the chance to say it. . . .

John Thomas Rourke had tried the two new firearms on the base range, and he was satisfied that these replicas were so close to the originals on which they were based as to be identical. He realized he did not even think of them as replicas, but rather as what they were intended to be.

The H-K 91 was always his preference in a semi-automatic rifle, but in the days Before The Night Of The War, he had chosen the CAR-15 because of ammunition, magazine, and parts compatibility with the military issue M-16. That was no longer a consideration.

216

The H-K 91 was no match for the Steyr-Mannlicher SSG as a sniper rifle, but for practical accuracy in a battle rifle, it was as good as any and better than most. He had no desire for the selective fire version. In the field, in the absence of supply trains, automatic weapons ate up too much ammunition.

The little twelve-inch-barreled Witness Protection 870 was a gun he had used — really only borrowed — on several occasions in the past. Nearly small enough to conceal as well as a long-barreled handgun, it was ultimately deadly in the proper hands at close range.

He had chosen these two firearms to add to his permanent battery, based not only on his needs for the impending raid, but on a future that — if he lived long enough — he knew would take him back to Eden, perhaps even to Eden City. To restore real life to Sarah, he had to get to Deitrich Zimmer.

His motto had always been "Plan ahead," and yet, beyond the moments when Sarah was restored and he executed Deitrich Zimmer and Martin Zimmer, eradicating their evil, he did not plan.

He knew his wife well. She would never accept as fact that Martin, the baby she had borne and nearly died over, was irredeemable and per force had himself to die. And she would never forgive him.

And he thought — he tried not to — about the other sleeper and why he slept: Wolfgang Mann. . . .

Annie dressed for her part. Costuming was not elaborate. But she didn't like it.

Longer skirts were comfortable. The wind could do what it liked, one could sit however one wished. But she was supposed to look unnoticeable, a woman's principal advantage in this work, as Natalia always said, so she had to dress the part. In these times, the typical woman of her age wore what she was wearing now.

217

She looked at herself in the mirror. Paul stood behind her and she didn't want to look at his face, just in case he laughed at her. She wore a grey sleeveless dress with a round collar, but its skirt barely covered her crotch. Her stockings, textured to produce a pattern of rosebuds, were black. Her boots, rising toward her shins, were white, high-heeled, plastic.

The only place she could hide a weapon was in her purse . . . and only one gun and a knife. She chose the Scoremaster .45 for the .45 ACP's authority over the larger capacity of her 9mm Beretta.

"You look sexy," Paul said from behind her.

She turned to face him, not knowing what to say.

"But I like you better the way you normally dress," he added.

And Annie put her arms around him and kissed him. . . .

Natalia's hair was loose, past her shoulders.

She wore a red sleeveless top, low cut in the front and back, a black miniskirt, and black high-heeled vinyl boots, which rose to her thighs. Her stockings were black fishnet.

"What do you think, Michael?"

"After this, you wear that only for me."

He was already dressed, in fatigue pants, a T-shirt, and a windbreaker. And he was weaponless, except for an energy pistol identical to those carried by the guards who were watching Martin Zimmer. . . .

John Rourke looked at himself in the mirror and laughed. Six centuries ago, he wouldn't have been caught dead in an aloha shirt. Flash had never been his style.

He slipped the double Alessi rig for the twin stainless Detonics mini guns on over it.

John Rourke still didn't like the way he looked.

* * *

Natalia Tiemerovna tapped the toe of her right boot, her eyes set on the exaggeratedly large face of her cheap plastic fashion watch.

She was down to three weapons, her Walther PPK/S with its suppressor down the small of her back, tucked into the waistband of her skirt. Her knife, the Bali-Song, was between her breasts. In her purse was the SIG-Sauer P-226. She'd tried it at the base range, putting two hundred 115-grain jacketed hollow points through it almost as fast as she could pull the trigger after she'd tested the pistol for accuracy.

The SIG — she thought of it as that, not a reproduction — worked.

She'd watched John, methodically testing his rifle, then the shotgun.

She still loved him, but not in the way she loved Michael. She'd never loved anyone that way.

If she died, she'd experienced the best of life.

And she waited now outside Pearl Harbor's security headquarters. For Annie.

So they could go for a walk together. . . .

Michael Rourke had never driven an ordinary car. A truck, yes, various tanks, and even staff cars that had all-terrain capabilities. But never an ordinary passenger car.

This one was electric, which was what most private ownership vehicles were these days.

He drove the car down a wide, palm-lined street, toward a place that was named after a dour-faced black naval officer from one hundred twenty-five years ago.

Maybe Mr. Sebastian, if there was a Heaven, would watch out for him in this place that bore his name . . . maybe . . .

* * *

The windbreaker was slightly long, but it had to be to accommodate the Witness Protection shotgun.

John Rourke waited as he saw the helicopter gunship coming in toward the pad.

As the machine neared, he recognized the pilot who was at its controls.

Emma Shaw.

He would never tell her, but he liked her, too. A lot.

Chapter Forty

Video screen billboards showed his picture—actually, Martin's picture—warning people in English, German (which he could read slightly) and Chinese (which he could not read at all) to be on the lookout for this dangerous armed fugitive, not naming the fugitive at all. That would have been awkward, since the real Martin Zimmer was the head of state of a foreign power of considerable influence.

He drove the car, an ordinary electrically powered sedan, along the palm-lined drive that followed the coastline, taking it toward Sebastian's Reef. He wore only one electronic device, that rather cleverly—he thought so, at least—concealed within the skeletonized belt holster for his supposedly stolen energy pistol. Once the pistol was drawn from the holster, the beeper would begin to transmit.

He had little faith in the energy pistol's effectiveness in any event and had no intention of drawing it until he needed to activate the signal. Reholstering would have no effect on the signal. It would still transmit. He was counting on being disarmed when he encountered the saboteurs at Sebastian's Reef. If he were not, he would discard the weapon and be able to get away with it, since it was contrary to Martin Zimmer's behavior patterns to go armed.

Michael Rourke kept driving. . . .

John Thomas Rourke's eyes followed the terrain below

them, the coastline, white surf edging brilliantly blue waves. His ears followed Emma Shaw's words. "All six helicopters are ready to go at the moment they're called up. One of the six is specially equipped to handle bomb disposal should that be necessary."

"Their explosives shouldn't be armed," Rourke told her, matter-of-factly. "Your father seems like a nice guy."

"He is. You'll have to meet my brother. In fact, you will. He's on dad's Tac Team."

"What's his name?"

"Eddie . . . but if you call him that, he'll get all bent out of shape. He likes Ed . . . thinks it sounds more manly or something."

"There used to be a television show about a talking horse named Ed," Rourke offered.

"A talking horse?"

"Just one of the many cultural highlights of Twentieth Century civilization, Emma. There was even a talking car who was somebody's mother come back from the dead."

Emma Shaw's voice dropped slightly in his headset. "My mom died when I was twelve."

"So you wound up mothering your dad and your brother?"

"Something like that," she said, her voice brightening a little. "You've got two fine kids, Michael and Annie."

"Two fine ones and one rotten one, Martin," Rourke responded.

"I hope you work this out. I mean, I don't know—"

"I don't think Martin's going to wake up some morning and decide to change his life, if that's what you mean. He's a racist, he's totally ruthless in his treatment of people— women in particular, it seems—and he's obsessed with the acquisition of power. That's closer to a description of Hitler than Albert Schweitzer, I'm afraid."

"He was that doctor who went off into the jungles and helped the natives. Started the Nobel Prize?"

"No, if memory serves, he received it once. The Nobel Prize was started because Alfred Nobel, the inventor of dynamite, was 'bent out of shape,' as you put it a moment ago, about the idea that his brilliant invention was being used to make war."

"You know a lot."

"Just different stuff. I'm a doctor of medicine. I couldn't practice today if I tried. If this is ever over, I'll have to remedy that." Then Rourke took his eyes from the coastline and looked at Emma Shaw. "What about you? What are you going to do after you get your twenty in? Or is it thirty these days?"

"It's still twenty, but you can do thirty. Some people do forty. I don't know. Maybe teach people how to fly. I don't know, really. I hear that in China there's a lot of opportunity for private aviation. The country's so vast and there are so few roads."

"Sounds like it'd be fun," Rourke smiled.

"Yeah, it does," she answered, glancing toward him for an instant. "What I . . . er . . . said when we were—"

"Don't worry about it," John Rourke said honestly.

"But I meant it." Rourke just looked at her. Emma no longer looked at him but continued speaking, her voice coming into his ear through the headset he wore. "I mean, I know you'd never give it a second thought, but I had to say it."

"Thank you," Rourke told her.

"You're welcome."

And he understood how she meant that.

Chapter Forty-One

John Rourke watched Tim Shaw's face as the Tac Team leader spoke into the microphone of his headset. "Ed . . . you got everybody into position? Over."

Rourke could not hear the incoming.

"All right. Soon as we get the signal, we move to ready position. Remember, be quick. Shaw out."

Lieutenant Commander Washington stepped in at the back of the truck. "My people are in place, Inspector."

"You goin' then?"

"On my way," Washington nodded.

Rourke said, "I'm joining you. Tim, hold the good thought."

Shaw nodded as Rourke caught up his windbreaker and slipped it on over the aloha shirt and the weapons, then stepped out into the mid-morning sunlight. Washington wore civies, blue jeans, and a sweatshirt. Rourke fell in beside him as they left the truck—a power company repair van—and started across the street toward the car.

The car, an Edison Seven, was electric, reminiscent in shape to a much-streamlined Corvette, low and flat at the nose and stubbed off at the rear end. He had been told it would top a hundred easily.

They stopped beside the car.

A cool wind was blowing in off the ocean, less than a mile distant from here, but the sun itself felt warm on Rourke's face and hands.

Washington extended his hand. "Good luck, Doctor."

"You guys take it easy," Rourke nodded, taking the black officer's hand in his.

Then John Rourke opened the door of the car and dropped behind the wheel.

There was no key, just a start code combination that he punched out on something which looked similar to a Twentieth Century touch-tone pad from a telephone.

There was a gentle hum. As Rourke touched his foot to the accelerator, the hum increased almost imperceptibly. He'd been briefed on the car, given a chance to try it on one of the roads winding through the base, but he still wasn't totally comfortable with something that didn't utilize an internal combustion engine.

There was a floor-mounted transmission — the concepts of manual or automatic were obsolete these days. He set the indicator to drive, then pulled away from the curb. . . .

Michael Rourke pulled up to the gates and honked his horn.

Video cameras — very small — moved into position.

He watched them.

The gates opened.

Michael Rourke drove the little electric car through the opening. He watched in the rearview mirror as the gates closed behind him. . . .

Natalia stepped out of the car, her legs looking impossibly long with the super short skirt and thigh-high boots. Annie got out of the car as well.

The hood latch release was already pulled and they both walked to the front of the car and, together, elevated the hood, looking inside the "engine" compartment. There was a smallish power plant, so small it would have fit into a large shoulder bag. There were two batteries, these about the size of standard automotive batteries like the one on the truck at The Retreat.

There was nothing wrong with the car, but from a distance nobody would know that. Annie sneaked a look over her shoulder.

Across the street were the gates leading into the compound's main driveway. If the two stranded women in short skirts routine worked, Annie knew, those gates might open. . . .

Paul Rubenstein pushed himself up and began to move through the woods that were just beyond the northernmost fence line of the estate. Police Sergeant Ed Shaw was beside him, the rest of the Tac Team personnel spread out in the trees on both sides of them.

The Schmiesser was tight in Paul's hands.

But he thought of Michael.

Less than thirty seconds ago, Ed Shaw's father called on the radio. Then Ed Shaw whispered, "We have the signal. And it's strong. Move to ready position now. Move to ready!"

Michael was inside.

That the signal was strong meant Michael was inside. That the signal was activated meant the gun Michael wore was withdrawn from its holster, either by Michael or by someone else.

The fence line was barely in sight. Before they reached it, they would stop again and wait, because there were video cameras surrounding the property. And the moment Paul Rubenstein, Sergeant Ed Shaw, and the Honolulu Tac Team approached within range of the cameras — the estate had its own power generators and so there was no way to kill power to the cameras — the thing would be started.

Inside his thin black leather gloves — they were real leather, not one of the modern synthetics — Paul Rubenstein's hands sweated.

Natalia's earrings were large. The left one was particularly heavy, being a receiver. She heard the voice of Inspector Shaw saying, "The stew is in the pot. I say again, the stew is in the pot."

Natalia stood up, no longer looking into the engine compartment. She smoothed down what little there was of her skirt with the tips of her fingers. Annie looked into her eyes. Natalia simply said, "Michael's inside."

Annie licked her lips and her face went a little pale. . . .

John Rourke pulled the little receiver out of his ear and flung it down on the seat.

Michael.

John turned down the relatively narrow street. Natalia and Annie were clearly visible standing beside the upraised hood of their car.

John pulled over in front of them and shut off the engine.

He stepped out of the car.

Natalia and Annie were trying to look slinky as they waved to him.

As he closed the door, John caught a glimpse of himself in the driver's side sport mirror. The lifemask that was constructed over his face, the blond hair dye and the blond mustache, the contact lenses to change eye color . . . it all worked. He didn't look like John Rourke.

He turned, looking at Natalia and his daughter. "What is the problem, girls?"

"Our car. It just died!" Annie called back in a rather squeaky voice.

"Let me take a look," Rourke responded, not so overly loud that it would appear obvious to any audio sensing equipment on the gates.

And he didn't even look at the gates. It was showtime. . . .

* * *

Michael Rourke walked along a narrow corridor, the walls and ceiling made of marble or something that resembled it, antique-style light fixtures hung along its length at regular intervals.

Six men walked with him, two in front, two behind, and one on either side of him.

They should have been more impressed that he was Martin Zimmer, should have treated him more deferentially. When they searched him, taking the "stolen" energy pistol, they were almost rude to him.

As Michael neared the end of the corridor—there was a set of double doors, resembling real wood—he had a disturbing thought, a very disturbing thought.

Croenberg managed the sabotage teams for the SS.

What if once Croenberg learned that Martin Zimmer was taken to Hawaii, he had told his people—quietly, of course—that Martin should die?

A sick feeling started in the pit of Michael Rourke's stomach.

He lied to himself that it was because he hadn't had much for breakfast. . . .

John Rourke stared up into the nearest video camera. The sun felt positively hot.

The camera turned toward his face.

John Rourke spoke to it in his best German accent. "I was wondering if it would be possible to have some assistance." He didn't say anything else, just stared into the camera.

A small speaker concealed within the grillwork abutting a stone pillar on Rourke's end of the metal gates came to life. "This is a private residence. You are trespassing."

Rourke smiled, looking down toward his feet, then back at the security camera. "I am standing in your driveway. This is trespassing?"

The voice—human, not prerecorded—repeated, "This is a private residence. You are trespassing."

"Is this the way you treat all visitors to your glorious Ha-

228

waii? You would not be treated in such a manner in New Germany, I assure you. I require assistance for the two young women on the other side of the street."

"Use your car phone."

"All I require is a pair of pliers, yes? Then I can fix the Fräuleins' car, yes?"

"Use your car phone to call for assistance."

John Rourke lit a cigarette with a modern disposable lighter, which he pocketed, blowing smoke toward the camera. "No."

"What do you mean, 'no'?"

John Rourke looked back toward the street, then into the camera lens. "These young women have been waiting here for quite some time. You did not notice them? Ha! I drive a rented automobile. There are no tools. The Fräuleins have no tools in their car, either. You will allow me the use of a pair of pliers, I think. Or I will stand here."

"Stand the fuck in the street, but get off the driveway or we will call the police."

"Then call the police. And I will call the embassy. I will call the newspapers and the television stations. Let us see how much privacy you have then, humph!"

There was no response.

John Rourke stood his ground. . . .

Michael Rourke was led through the doorway, the doors opening automatically. He imagined they were controlled by some sort of electronic eye apparatus. Too much was electronic these days, he reflected.

Beyond the doorway was a large desk.

There were several computer and video screens arrayed on it, a central control panel and, behind the desk, a solitary man. He stood up. "Herr Zimmer! This is a true honor, sir!"

Michael decided it was time for his Martin Zimmer-the-prick act. "What is the meaning of this! I demand these ruffians be dismissed and—"

The man behind the desk—backlit by the window, Michael could not see his face—started to laugh. And he kept laughing.

Michael Rourke didn't think the situation was shaping up to be funny at all. . . .

Ed Shaw's voice was a low rasp. "Once we get the signal from Dr. Rourke, Mr. Rubenstein, we move. Hang in there."

"Jamming the video signal's going to buy us about sixty seconds at best," Paul noted.

"In sixty seconds, we can be over the fence. They'll know they've been penetrated—or suspect it at least—but not by how many. Their motion detectors won't be sensitive enough to give them any numbers. But we should pull most of their security attention to the rear of the property, so Dr. Rourke and the others can do their number."

"This sucks," Paul observed. Helicopters would have been spotted as they came in. The high altitude overflight photos the Navy arranged for and the video taken when Emma Shaw flew John near the place indicated a sophisticated aerial surveillance net around the place.

The security here was extraordinarily good, and the plan was built around turning the security system against itself rather than attempting to disarm it or get around it, both of which would have been impossible.

Six choppers were waiting but would not go up unless he or John gave the word, all in the name of diplomacy. Since Martin Zimmer's face was not generally known outside the leadership circle of Eden, it could be argued that when the Rourke Family brought him to Hawaii, it was not realized he was a foreign head of state.

The raid on the compound could be written off as overzealous police work in response to a tip.

Even Lieutenant Commander Washington and his SEAL team personnel were in civvies, all of them armed with false Honolulu PD Tac Team credentials. Once concrete evidence, which could be taken to Trans-Global Alliance headquarters in Switzerland, was found in the house and the intended sabotage could be proven, then the military could act. Diplomatic concerns would go by the board.

Paul Rubenstein just hoped that Michael Rourke wouldn't die because of diplomatic concerns. . . .

"You are still standing in the driveway."

"Americans may be rude, but Gott in Himmel they are perceptive!"

"This is the last time I will ask you to leave."

John Rourke smiled into the camera. "Zer gut—then you will bring the pliers, yes?"

There was a long pause, then the voice from the speaker said, "All right, damnit!"

"Danke!"

John Rourke lit another cigarette, wishing it were a cigar. . . .

Michael was made to sit in a chair facing the light, on the opposite side of the desk. The man's face became visible as he stepped away from the window, crossing the room toward a small bar on the far wall.

The room itself was luxurious in the extreme—or seemed so at least. Aside from the large video screens on the wall, flanking the bar, it could have been a Twentieth Century boardroom or something like it, judging by the video movies Michael had seen at The Retreat and descriptions he'd read of such places in books.

When the man reached the bar, he turned around.

Now Michael could see his face. He almost wished he couldn't. The face, deeply suntanned, was so skinny that it appeared skeletal, the eyes bulging slightly. The lips, thin and long, were drawn back over stark white teeth.

"Martin Zimmer, our leader!" The man's right hand shot forward in a Nazi salute. Then he laughed. "Strutting fool!

231

Did you think that the SS would follow such as you! You have walked into your own death, I am afraid. Have a drink, yes?" The man turned away and poured some whiskey-colored liquid from a decanter. "You may not remember me, Herr Zimmer. But we did meet once, in Eden City. Gruppenführer Croenberg introduced us. If memory serves, you drank vodka."

With that, he set down the decanter from which he'd just poured, then took an ordinary bottle filled with clear liquid. He twisted open the cap and poured into a second glass.

He turned around, a glass in each hand, smiled again, and said, "I am Sturmbannführer Luther Schmidt." He walked back across the room, his long-legged stride easy, confident. He extended the hand holding the glass of vodka. Michael took it. "A toast then, Herr Zimmer," and Schmidt raised his glass. "To the new Reich and to its new leadership

Michael didn't raise his glass. He studied the surface of the liquid, then Schmidt's dark, penetrating eyes. There was laughter in them.

Schmidt said, "You will be shot to death, with an American weapon, of course, and left to be found. The Americans will be charged with causing the death of Eden's beloved leader. The people of Eden, the party membership, all will mourn this tragic death. All will be united in their resolve to take revenge against the Trans-Global Alliance. You will be of greater benefit to our ultimate victory in your death than would ever have been possible in life for you."

Michael decided to say something. "Would it do any good to—"

"To beg?" Schmidt laughed.

Michael said, "No, just to remind you that you'll never get away with this? I know what I'm talking about."

Schmidt laughed again, but otherwise made no response.

Michael Rourke decided he was definitely in trouble. . . .

John Rourke saw the car—more like a Twentieth Century

golf cart in size—moving along the driveway, a lone man sitting in it. Rourke glanced across the street toward Natalia and Annie. "Fräulein, if you would, take the pliers from this fellow. I will begin to make the repair." Rourke left the streetside of the driveway and crossed over, aware that the surveillance cameras probably still had him in view. Natalia was already walking toward the gates. As they passed each other in the middle of the street, Rourke winked and whispered, "Here we go."

Natalia walked past, as if nothing had transpired between them. . . .

Natalia Tiemerovna's thoughts were on Michael. She told herself that if he were in immediate danger, Annie would have known somehow.

She watched as the golf cart-sized vehicle began to slow, nearing the fence. Natalia stepped closer to the fence, hunching her shoulders so her cleavage would deepen.

The golf cart stopped.

The man—he was in his middle twenties or so, blond, blue-eyed, muscular, and tanned under a short-sleeved white knit shirt—stepped out. "Where's the German?" Evidently, his question was answered as she followed his eyes across the street. "I guess you get these," he said, moving nearer to the fence, the pliers in his hand. He was visibly armed, a shoulder holster with some small pistol in it under his left arm. The pliers were in his right hand.

"You're just so nice to help us," Natalia smiled.

"He was making himself a pain in the ass, girlie. Here." He extended the pliers through the fence.

Natalia did two things.

She twisted the ornament on the strap of her purse, sending a radio signal to Paul and the Tac Team to activate the jamming of the video security system, then grabbed the blond man's wrist with her right hand and jerked him toward her so his face slammed into the fence.

Her left hand twisted behind her, freeing the suppressor-fitted PPK/S from the small of her back, its safety already off. She interposed her body between the camera and the man, in case the system weren't already jammed. But she knew it would be. She put the muzzle of the pistol to the blond man's throat in the next instant and pulled the trigger. . . .

John Rourke slammed down the hood on the car that Natalia and Annie drove, then ran for his own car. He threw open the driver's side door, then jumped behind the wheel. Behind him, in the rearview mirror, he saw Annie already behind the wheel of the other car, which started into motion. John Rourke punched the ignition code of his own car. In about a second, he'd know if the Edison Seven had any guts or was just a pretty face. . . .

Natalia stabbed the detonator into the plastique and ran, the remote that would activate it in her left hand, her PPK/S in her right. John's car was in high-speed reverse down the street, while Annie was making a three-point turn.

Natalia, in the middle of the street, pushed the button on the remote.

She kept running, hearing pieces of the gates whistling through the air behind her. . . .

Paul Rubenstein and Ed Shaw reached the fence simultaneously, three of the Tac Team men activating the tactical ascender. It was similar to a ladder, but the rungs were more like actual step treads, segmented, pneumatically operating. As the ladder segments shot upward, the entire mechanism leaned forward, supports folding out automatically in front, supporting the ascender.

Shaw started up the treads, Paul Rubenstein behind him.

234

The platform was already folding out from the top.

Once they reached the platform, they would jump. . . .

Schmidt had a gun, one that Michael Rourke respected.

The gun, most likely a Lancer reproduction but identical in appearance to a Walther P-38K 9mm Parabellum, was pointed at his head.

The six men who had accompanied him into Schmidt's office were running to their posts.

A loud, piercing alarm was sounding from the corridor, the doors open.

Michael Rourke figured he had nothing to lose, so he jumped toward Schmidt and the gun.

Chapter Forty-Two

John Rourke stomped the Edison Seven's accelerator pedal to the floor and, reassuringly, the machine shot forward into the driveway. The body of the man Natalia had shot lay there, causing Rourke to steer around it.

From the hedgerow on both sides of the drive, energy weapons began firing, blue-white streaks flashing on all sides of him, apparently part of some automatic intruder defense system. "Shit," Rourke rasped. He cut the wheel left, toward the hedgerow. An energy bolt impacted across the hood of the Edison Seven, the windshield spiderwebbing, the synth-glass blackening. Rourke kept driving, the Edison Seven picking up speed as it crashed through the hedgerow, where a fence was hidden within. The car hesitated for an instant, then there was the sound of metal tearing metal, pieces of the fence flying away on either side of the Edison Seven's low-swept hood.

There were more of the energy bolts now, but from behind him. And, in the rearview mirror, he could see Annie and Natalia's car crashing through the same opening in the hedge.

The grassy strip between the two driveways was dry and hard.

John Rourke was thrown up and down and sideways, despite the seat restraint he wore. Nevertheless, he was able to steer the Edison Seven toward the fountain at the far end of the strip, in the arc of the horseshoe driveway.

* * *

Michael Rourke's left hand was over the Walther P-38K. His right hand, balled into a fist, crossed Schmidt's lantern-shaped jaw at the same instant the pistol discharged.

Michael's left hand stung, his flesh caught in the slide, the bullet pinging off the desk.

Michael started to reach for the pistol, but Schmidt's left caught him in the abdomen, doubling him forward. Schmidt's hands grabbed for Michael's left hand and wrist. Michael felt a sharp pain. Schmidt turned around, flipping Michael forward into a roll, throwing him hard to the floor.

A chunk of flesh from the web of Michael's left hand was missing, blood spurting out between his thumb and first finger. The gun discharged, a bullet impacting the floor beside Michael as he rolled. Getting to his feet, the body blocked Schmidt, throwing his left shoulder with the full force of his weight against his opponent's chest. The Walther flew from Schmidt's right hand as he and Michael fell to the floor. Michael's right knee struck the ground hard and his right leg went numb. His left fist hammered upward, catching Schmidt under the jaw, twisting the man's head back.

Schmidt's right knee smashed upward, missing Michael's testicles, impacting the pelvic bone instead. Michael's breath left him in a rush. But he lurched forward and downward, his left elbow arcing across Schmidt's face, glancing off the right cheekbone and the nose.

Schmidt's nose was broken. As blood sprayed, Michael averted his eyes.

Schmidt's voice was a low growl, "Damn you, Zimmer!"

Michael's elbow thrust back, missing Schmidt's nose and mouth, impacting him across the forehead. Michael hissed, "I'm not Zimmer, asshole. I'm Michael Rourke!"

Schmidt's left fist seemed to come from nowhere. Michael twisted his head away but too late, the right side of his jaw taking a punch that came so hard and fast floaters started across his eyes and he fell away.

237

Schmidt was up. His right foot snapped out, Michael's hands going to his groin and his knees locking together as Schmidt kicked. Michael caught the ankle and rolled, pulling Schmidt down to the floor on top of him.

As Schmidt fell, his left knee raised and his body weight crashed down against his opponent, its full force concentrated in the knee at the center of Michael's abdomen.

Michael lost his breath and started to vomit in the same instant. He groped upward with his right hand, grabbing part of Schmidt's left ear, then ripping. The middle knuckles of Michael's left hand were formed into a wedge that he snapped upward toward Schmidt's larynx, to crush it, to kill. Schmidt dodged, falling away, Michael ripping part of his left ear as he screamed.

Then Schmidt was up.

Michael staggered to his feet, half doubled over, unable to stand fully erect, vomit mixed with blood dripping from his mouth.

Schmidt's left hand moved and suddenly there was a knife in it. "Michael Rourke, then. Die!" And Schmidt hurtled himself forward. . . .

The Edison Seven skidded, its rear end fishtailing right, the car sliding broadside through the hedge at the far end of the greenway and into the arc of the horseshoe-shaped driveway.

Energy weapons were not in evidence here, but there was a fence, the Edison Seven splitting it, pieces of metal spraying outward, the passenger side windows shattering.

The car skidded sideways, toward the fountain that was at the approximate midpoint between the hedgerow and the steps leading into the building.

John Rourke threw open the driver's side door, tore off his seat restraints, and hurled himself out as he grabbed for the rifle case beneath the seat. He hit the gravel hard, going into a roll.

As his body slammed to a halt, the Edison Seven crashed into the fountain, collapsing the near side of the bowl surrounding it, electricity arcing off the hood as energy weapons were fired from the steps by at least two men.

John Rourke's right hand snaked crossbody, snatching one of the twin stainless Detonics mini guns from the double Alessi shoulder holster. He punched the pistol forward, firing a double tap toward the steps. There were three men on the steps now, one of them falling down dead, the second and third running back inside the building.

Rourke safed the pistol as he got to his feet, shoving the .45 into the waistband of his trousers while he unlimbered the H-K 91. He racked the action back with his left hand.

He was up, running toward the car. He ducked behind the car, at an angle to the house so any projectiles fired toward him would have the maximum amount of metal to penetrate before reaching him. . . .

Michael Rourke's father had always taught him, "In a knife fight, if you have to, take the cut on the outside of the forearm. Less chance of bleeding to death or sustaining incapacitation."

As Schmidt's knife arced outward and downward, there was nothing else Michael could do but block it with his left forearm, to avoid taking a cut across his abdomen.

As the blade crossed his flesh, Michael Rourke shrieked with pain and anger, blood spurting from his arm as his right hand snapped forward, inside his opponent's guard, the heel going for the base of Schmidt's nose . . . to break it . . . drive the bone upward through the ethmoid bone and into the brain . . . to kill.

Michael's blow missed, hitting the front teeth instead. There was a spray of blood as Schmidt's lips split and he fell back.

Schmidt still held the knife.

Michael's left forearm was drenched with blood, and he could not take another cut like that.

His face a bloody mask, Schmidt charged forward, the knife held high in a rapier hold, aimed for Michael's chest.

Michael Rourke waited.

At the last second he dared, he dropped right, Michael's legs scissoring outward, catching Schmidt's feet and bringing his out-of-balance body crashing downward. Michael rolled onto his chest and pushed up, nearly collapsed. He was getting light-headed now from the blood loss and pain.

But he stood, sagging forward.

He was near the bar.

The decanter. It looked like real glass, not synth-glass. If it was . . .

Schmidt was on his feet. Holding the knife as he had before, he charged, cursing in German.

Michael's right hand had the decanter, his left the synth-glass bottle of vodka.

As Schmidt came for him, Michael sidestepped, swinging the bottle of vodka outward and toward Schmidt's head, the synth-glass bottle impacting his head so hard that it cracked.

Schmidt staggered.

Michael held the whiskey decanter by its base and smashed it against the bar rail.

There was a reassuring sound of glass breaking.

Schmidt fell forward against the bar, started to turn.

Michael still held the cracked vodka bottle, the liquor dribbling through the crack and down his nearly useless left arm, the alcohol burning him.

With all of his weight behind the vodka bottle, Michael crashed it downward across Schmidt's right forearm. Then Michael stepped in, holding the smashed whiskey decanter by the neck, near his right shoulder, arcing downward.

Schmidt's shredded lips drew back in a snarl.

Michael was losing consciousness, the pain in his left arm incredible now.

His right hand swept outward.

Schmidt's right hand still held the knife, driving it upward for Michael's abdomen.

Michael's right hand arced right to left.

There was a look in Schmidt's eyes for a micro second.

In that look, Michael Rourke saw that Schmidt realized death was coming.

The jagged base of the whiskey decanter slashed across Schmidt's throat, choking a scream from his bloodied lips.

Michael's body was carried on his own momentum and he started to fall, a wash of darkness flooding over him. . . .

Paul Rubenstein ran dead out, Ed Shaw and the other Tac Team personnel surrounding him. Gunfire, both conventional and energy weapons, emanated from the rear of the house, more than Paul had expected.

And he made a decision.

"Drop! Drop!"

Paul threw himself down to the ground, the others around him doing the same, returning fire to the rear of the house.

On their immediate right were the stables, a large exercise corral beside it. Between the stables and the house lay the enormous garage he'd seen in the aerial photos. Gunfire came from the deck on the near side of the garage as well.

They were pinned down.

He activated the signal, calling in the unmarked helicopters with Lieutenant Commander Washington's civie-clad SEAL team aboard. . . .

Annie Rubenstein hit the brakes, causing the car to skid off the grass into the hedge, coming to a dead stop just short of the Edison Seven her father had driven. She could see him disappearing through the doorway and into the house.

Beside Annie, Natalia was already pulling on a flak jacket as she slid out the passenger side, Annie sliding out the same way after her. Annie grabbed her flak jacket from under the back seat cushion, the jacket longer than her miniskirt. Under the seat cushion as well were two of the short-barreled German assault weapons. Natalia handed her one, along with a musette bag loaded with magazines. "Ready? You take the left, I'll take the right."

Annie was up, running as fast as she could with the stupid-looking boots and their higher-than-normal heels, almost stumbling in the gravel driveway.

But she reached the steps on the right side.

As she looked, Natalia was on the left side.

They gave each other a nod, then started off, Annie following the building's perimeter along the right side. . . .

John Rourke made a decision. There was a heavy concentration of gunfire coming from the rear of the house. If Paul hadn't already called in added personnel, he would. He activated the signaling device that was clipped to his belt.

Diplomacy be damned.

Rourke moved along the wall of a large entrance hall, rectangular in shape, the ceiling extending upward through the second floor.

A balcony traversed it from one side of the house to the other, and as Rourke looked he saw movement on the near side.

Rourke tucked back into a doorway opening, checking on the inside as he did. A man's shape appeared from behind an overturned table and fired an energy weapon, the blue-white bolt of electricity impacting the door frame, flames

242

licking upward. Rourke pulled away, firing the H-K 91 from the hip, catching the man with the energy weapon in center of mass, flipping him back against the wall.

The movement he had seen a second before along the balcony appeared to be three men, clearly visible now, running from the near side of the balcony toward the other side of the second floor.

Rourke had the H-K 91 to his shoulder and fired. . . .

Natalia Tiemerovna advanced along the wall of the building. There was sporadic gunfire from inside, but there was a heavier concentration, sounding like enough for a small war, emanating from the rear of the house. . . .

Michael Rourke opened his eyes and vomit rose in his throat.

There was heavy gunfire from the rear of the house, some from within the building. He spat the vomit onto the carpet. He was light-headed and sick from the loss of blood. With some difficulty, he rolled onto his right side, keeping his left arm elevated in that manner, hopefully slowing the flow.

His trousers were beltless, the plastic holster he'd worn for the miserable little energy pistol a clip-on style. He wore a T-shirt and windbreaker, no tie.

"Shit," he groaned.

His eyes traveled to the dead body lying beside him. Schmidt's gun, a P-38K. Worn in a shoulder holster? Michael Rourke pushed with his feet and pulled with his right hand, dragging himself toward Schmidt's body. The Nazi's bony face had a slightly waxy look to it, but Michael realized this was mostly his imagination; Schmidt hadn't been dead that long. Michael started to reach under the blood-drenched coat to search for a shoulder holster harness, but

243

his hand stopped. Schmidt wore a belt, easier to access and easier to utilize for his purpose.

The fingers of Michael's right hand felt thick and stiff; clumsy, but he managed to undo the belt buckle. Then he braced one foot against Schmidt's chest as he pulled, freeing the belt, falling back as he did so.

Michael managed to sit up, his head swimming with the sudden movement. The belt. He began to wrap it around his arm, between the wound and his heart. . . .

Paul Rubenstein fired the Schmiesser from his shoulder, catching two of the men on the garage's sun deck, one of them careening over the balcony. He started running again, along with Ed Shaw and five of the TAC team, moving in a low crouch, their weapons firing alternately toward the house and toward the garage. As of yet, the helicopters were not in sight, but time was becoming critical, so the reinforcements were a luxury they could not afford.

Shaw shouted to one of his men, "Use your grenade launcher, Jake! On that sun deck! Hurry!"

There was a whooshing sound, Paul Rubenstein ducking involuntarily as the grenade whistled over him. It arced downward now, and as it hit the sun deck, the near end of the open structure seemed to dissolve within the explosion's fireball. . . .

John Rourke ran along a long corridor, at the end of which was a room, the doors wide open. But there were single-doored rooms on either side of the corridor, and despite the speed with which Rourke moved, he was cautious as he went from doorway to doorway.

Halfway along the corridor's length, doors opened on either side. Men armed with German assault rifles of the type Natalia had been using recently jumped out, opening

244

fire. Rourke threw his left shoulder against a doorway just past, the door rocking inward under his weight as he went through in a roll, coming up on his knees. There was no one in the room.

Rourke moved toward the wall separating him from the next room. He reached under his windbreaker, on the opposite side from the sling for the Witness Protection shotgun, freeing one of the small plastique charges. . . .

His arm wound in an improvised tourniquet, Michael Rourke lurched toward the windows behind the desk. The P-38K Schmidt he had used was in his right hand, a fresh eight-round magazine up the well, the partially spent one pocketed.

As he parted sheer curtains, he could see through the windows helicopter gunships coming in, over the trees beyond the house. Men occupied positions of cover on a bricked patio, firing toward other men on the ground, storming toward the house. As of yet, no bullet had struck these windows, but it was only a matter of time.

The gun still in his hand, he rubbed his fingertips over the window. It felt like real glass.

He stuffed the pistol into his trouser band and reached for the desk chair. The chair was heavy, but he convinced himself he could lift it well enough to crash it through the window. . . .

Natalia reached the far end of the house, and as she did she saw a man. He saw her in the same instant, wheeling toward her with an energy pistol in each hand.

Natalia fired, two three-round bursts into his center of mass.

Then she threw herself over the hedge and to the ground.

245

More men were coming around the side of the house, firing toward her. . . .

John Rourke set the detonator to ten seconds, then ran back across the room, dropping behind a sofa, drawing his body up into a fetal position in order to protect bare skin.

His hands covering his ears, the concussion from the small charge of plastique was still incredibly loud. As the sound started to abate, Rourke was up, the air in the room clouded with plaster dust, a hole in the far wall.

Rourke ran toward it, the H-K 91 in both hands.

As he reached the opening, the man who had fired at him from the doorway was picking himself up, raising his weapon.

John Rourke fired first, two rounds, one to the chest and the other to the head, the man's body flying back against the doorjamb.

Rourke advanced to the doorway, a rifle raised toward him from the door on the opposite side of the corridor. Rourke fired first, two rounds, throwing the man's body back into the room.

Rourke shifted the partially spent magazine out of the well, instead putting in the full one clipped to it.

He stepped to the doorway.

There was the sound of glass shattering from the room at the far end of the corridor.

Rourke ran toward the sound. . . .

Michael Rourke pushed the muzzle of the P-38K through the shattered window and fired, the gun held almost at full extension of his arm. He put a single round into one of the house defenders just as the man turned toward the sound of breaking glass, Michael's bullet catching him in the left cheek, his nose exploding outward in a cloud of blood.

Michael swung the muzzle of his weapon, finding another target and firing, putting the man down.

In the hands of a third man, an assault rifle was coming on line toward his body. Michael fired a third time, a bullet into the man's throat.

Behind him, Michael Rourke heard the sound of his father's voice shouting, "Get down!"

Michael threw himself right, gunfire hammering toward him, what remained of the glass in the window shattering, raining down around him.

John Rourke grabbed for one of the plastique charges, flipping the detonator to five seconds, hurtling it left-handed through the shot-out window as he ran toward his son, throwing his body over Michael's. In the next instant, there was the concussion and the roar.

Rourke's left hand felt for a pulse. Weak, but steady. Michael was unconscious, not dead.

Rourke was up on his knees, the H-K 91 to his shoulder. As gunfire tore into the window frame, he fired, again and again and again, putting down man after man.

The H-K was empty, and Rourke buttoned out the clipped-together magazines, letting them fall to the glass surrounding him on the floor. As he rammed one of the two remaining spares up the rifle's magazine well, two of the house's defenders charged toward him. With the rifle in his left hand, Rourke grabbed for the Detonics mini gun at his waistband, the hammer cocked, the safety on. He thumbed down the safety and fired, one double tap to each man.

The slide locked open, empty, both men going down.

Rourke rammed the pistol into his belt, the H-K to his shoulder again, the chamber charged. He fired. . . .

Natalia Tiemerovna crawled along through the dirt,

247

dropping to cover behind an apron of concrete running up to the patio. Gunfire tore into the hedges near here, chipping the concrete as well.

She pushed the muzzle of the assault rifle up over the concrete and fired blindly, spraying the muzzle right and left. . . .

Annie Rubenstein reached the rear end of the house. . . .

There appeared to be an outdoor barbecue of red brick built here, about four feet high and closed on three sides. She took up a position beside it, shouldering her rifle, then opened fire on the defenders of the house.

John Rourke stepped over the window frame and down into the patio, the H-K tensioned on its sling so he could fire the rifle one-handed, his second Detonics mini gun in his left hand.

Men were trying to escape the patio now, but there was nowhere to run, helicopters coming in from the woods behind the house, some of Washington's civvies-clad SEAL team already out of the choppers and storming the house, more men coming.

Rourke fired out the Detonics pistol, stuffing it, slide open, into his waistband, firing the last three rounds from the H-K almost simultaneously with the last round from the .45.

He let the rifle fall to his side on its sling as he swept up one of the stubby-barreled German assault weapons from beside a dead body on the patio.

He fired out a long burst, then another and another, putting four more men down, a fifth throwing away his weapon and dropping to his knees, shouting in German, "I surrender! I surrender!"

Rourke approached him, threw down the spent assault rifle, and took up the man's weapon, then crossed the adversary's jaw with his left fist, knocking him unconscious, saving him for later. He couldn't leave the man awake behind him to change his mind.

Rourke crossed the patio toward a concrete apron extending away from the house, picking up another of the light-caliber, stubby-barreled German rifles.

A half-dozen men were charging toward a hedgerow about thirty yards away.

"Natalia," Rourke whispered.

From behind him, he heard Annie shouting, "Daddy! Natalia's over—"

"Cover my back!" Rourke ordered. He broke into a run, the rifle in his right hand going out with one burst, two bursts from the one in his left, three of the men down.

Rourke cast away both rifles, reaching under his windbreaker with both hands and freeing the Witness Protection shotgun slung there, racking the pump, the pistol grip butt at his right side.

He aimed his body toward the nearest of the men, not just fifteen yards away, firing, the shots going low, hitting the man in the kidneys rather than between the shoulder blades.

Rourke racked another double-O buck, pushing the shotgun out ahead of him, firing, tromboning the action, firing again as one of the men wheeled toward him and fired.

He saw Natalia on her feet behind the hedgerow. Her pistol and his shotgun discharged simultaneously, the man's body twisting, falling.

Natalia stepped out from behind the hedgerow, her left arm hanging limp at her side, dripping blood, her black stockings shredded over her thighs.

Rourke left the shotgun with an empty round in the chamber, shifted it under his left arm, and reached under his jacket to the small of his back, where he had a single double-magazine pouch.

He reloaded one of the Detonics Combatmasters, then the other, both pistols cocked and locked in his belt for an instant as he pocketed the last of the spent magazines.

Natalia approached.

He offered her the shotgun.

She shoved her pistol into the waistband of her skirt and took it.

Rourke handed her four loose shells from his pocket.

Her left arm moving slowly, she began inserting the shells beneath the action.

As he turned back toward the patio, he saw Annie, her assault rifle in one hand, her pistol in the other.

With both Detonics mini guns in his fists, Rourke started back to the patio.

He heard Natalia racking the shotgun.

Rourke turned in toward the house. A dozen or so of the men here, saboteurs sent to destroy from within, to soften for the attack, still returned fire from the grounds between the patio and the garage. Lieutenant Commander Washington's men and the Tac Team people, Paul with them, Rourke knew, seemed to be everywhere.

Rourke approached the house, peering through the shot-out window, then stepping over the sill. "Be careful of the broken glass," Rourke cautioned the two women.

He came upon Michael, examing him quickly but thoroughly. One major wound on his left forearm, a knife cut, tied off with a tourniquet. Blood loss. Shock.

Natalia—he wondered how she'd gotten over the window sill in her short skirt—was beside him. Rourke looked at her. "He'll be okay. Find something to keep him warm. Get the medics."

Annie was trying to get through the window but not doing a very good job of it with the broken glass all around the frame. Rourke set his pistols on the desk, reached through, and scooped his daughter up into his arms, setting her down inside the room. "Help Natalia with your brother. He'll be all right."

John Rourke picked up his pistols, then started across the room, back into the corridor.

There would be a room.

One special room.

There always was.

Chapter Forty-Three

On the way toward the basement—he knew there was one from the architectural plans—he acquired another assault rifle and loaded the magazine, with only four rounds remaining, into the action of his H-K.

The entrance to the basement was not easy to find but not all that difficult, either, since from historical data concerning the house as it was used while headquarters for the Trans-Global Alliance, he knew where the interior walls should be. When he found one that should not be there, he assumed—correctly—that it masked access to the basement.

After a moment, he found an electronic release and a panel opened, revealing a reasonably wide stairwell going straight downward.

Rourke took the stairs slowly, the twin stainless Detonics pistols, hammers lowered and chambers loaded, thrust into their holsters, the German assault rifle in his left hand, the semi-automatic H-K 91 in his right.

A man jumped into view at the base of the stairs, an energy pistol raised in his right hand. Rourke fired a burst from the little assault rifle, cutting the man down.

He reached the base of the stairs.

Another man was nearly through a metal door. Rourke shot him once with the H-K, the man's body collapsing between the door and the door frame, blocking it open.

Rourke approached the door, kicked it inward, and stepped aside.

"Do not kill us!"

Rourke said nothing.

Another voice. "We will tell you—"

Rourke shoved the muzzle of the H-K through the doorway. "Step into the open, hands in the air above your heads, nothing in your hands!"

Through the crack, he could see two men and a woman, all of them with empty hands raised.

Rourke took the chance, kicking the door inward all the way, stepping over the body and inside.

There was a fourth person in the room, a stack of computer disks on a table in front of him, the hum of a degausser from beside him. "Step away!" Rourke ordered.

The man wiped a disk across the degausser as he aimed a pistol toward Rourke.

John Rourke shot the man dead, the body sprawling over the table.

There were about twenty or thirty disks on the floor, but a stack of at least fifty or sixty were still on the table. Documents were heaped in the center of the floor, but no one had set them afire yet.

John Rourke looked at the walls. Maps, partially torn down. Computer terminals still showed map displays.

"Will you kill us?" It was the woman with her hands raised over her head—she was pretty in a severe sort of way—who asked him.

"No." In this room he had what he wanted—invasion plans, maps, lists of agents, almost certainly. "There's no reason now," John Rourke told her.

He safed the H-K, letting it fall to his side on its sling. He did the same with the little German assault rifle, but set that weapon on the table near him. He drew one of the twin stainless Detonics pistols with his right hand, with his left taking a thin, dark tobacco cigar from his shirt pocket, its end already cut. He found the battered old Zippo lighter in his pants pocket, lighting the cigar in its blue-yellow flame.

The woman—she still stood there with her hands raised—said, "You can never win. We will be victorious. Your cause is hopeless. You can never win!"

John Rourke smiled as he exhaled smoke through his nostrils, the cigar clamped tightly in his teeth. The fight was just beginning, but the Eden government and its Nazi allies were like a cancer on the face of an Earth given a second chance. A cancer was treated or killed or cut out, but never ignored. "We can win. Wait and see," John Rourke told them. "Wait and see, and we'll surprise you."

He began to tear away the lifemask from his face, and he noticed the woman's eyes. After a moment, she gasped, "It is John Rourke!"

After all, he thought, he had promised a surprise. But this wasn't it.